The Bishop's Horse Race

The Bishop's HorseRace

Blaine M. Yorgason
Brenton G. Yorgason

Bookcraft
Salt Lake City, Utah

Library of Congress Catalog Card Number: 79-54894
ISBN O-88494-385-2

3rd Printing, 1980

Lithographed in the United States of America
PUBLISHERS PRESS
Salt Lake City, Utah

Contents

Introduction

The setting for *The Bishop's Horse Race* is Utah Territory in the summer of 1888. Historically, besides the entire nation being hotter than a burnt boot, the eastern United States was still recovering financially from a devastating late-spring blizzard. Benjamin Harrison had just been nominated by the Republicans to run against Grover Cleveland, Louisa May Alcott had died, and Belva Ann Lockwood had been nominated for President of the United States by the Equal Rights Party at its convention in Des Moines, Iowa.

In Utah, where the great drought of the nineties was just beginning, the Mormon Church, whose President, John Taylor, had recently died in exile, was reeling under the Edmunds-Tucker Act. This act, passed by Congress the previous March, added to the Edmunds law of 1882 to provide that—

1. polygamy was a felony;
2. polygamy was the same as unlawful cohabitation;
3. no polygamist could vote;
4. no polygamist could hold public office;
5. no polygamist could serve on a jury;

6. The Church of Jesus Christ of Latter-day Saints was disincorporated;
7. the Perpetual Emigration Fund was dissolved;
8. female suffrage was abolished;
9. children of polygamous marriages were disinherited;
10. all Church funds and properties were escheated to the government.

In addition to the above, polygamists themselves reeled when two federal judges held that separate indictments could be brought against a polygamist for each and every time he appeared in the proximity of one of his wives. Some were fined over twenty thousand dollars each on separate three-hundred-dollar charges, all chalked up within the space of a few hours or days. The judges also ruled that wives had to testify against their husbands; they imprisoned those who refused; and they allowed the children to accompany their mothers to the pen, where all were classified as jailbirds. To combat this situation, Church leaders counseled the minority of their members who were living the law of plural marriage to hide out, and elaborate schemes, codes and hiding places were devised to enable members to avoid the long arm of what they considered to be an unjust law. The circumstances depicted in *The Bishop's Horse Race* occurred as a direct result of this atmosphere of fight and flight.

Besides polygamists and federal officials, there were several other elements in Utah in 1888, two of which figure in our story. Among the Mormons were many who were inactive, ''Jack-Mormons'' they were occasionally called. Many of these, not polygamist at all, found themselves suffering for a principle they weren't even involved in. To ease the pressure and to gain favor with the Feds, it was not infrequent for these people to ''spy'' on their polygamous neighbors, and occasionally to participate in the ''polyg hunts'' or ''cohab parties'' conducted by the territorial marshal and his deputies. These people, of course, caused the polygamists much distress.

The second of the two additional elements dealt with in the story is the outlaw element, those who were using the rugged country of Eastern Utah, known even then as Robber's Roost, as a hideout and base for their nefarious operations. These men quite naturally carried guns. But outlaws weren't the only ones who went around armed. In a land and a time when most men carried weapons, and when they were essential to survival, violence seemed almost to be a way of life. When weapons and duels were the accepted means of settling disputes, among Congressmen as well as among highwaymen, when the July 23, 1889, seventy-five-round bare-knuckle fight between John L. Sullivan and Jake Kilrain was billed as the world's greatest sporting event, and when violence, especially in the West, was so casual and off-hand, it is not surprising to learn that Mormons, too, occasionally dealt with each other in physical ways. The remarkable thing, when one considers the buffetings the Mormons received from those around and among them, is that as a people they restrained themselves as frequently and as well as they did.

Now to the story itself, which we hastily admit is fictitious in much of its detail. Still, it should be understood that the story is based upon actual experiences of men and women who recorded in their journals what they saw and felt. A man who was serving as a bishop actually did run his giant horse in such a race, and he ran it for the reasons specified in our story. The raid by the marshals is written as described by those who experienced it, the appearance of the strange old man was also recorded, President Taylor made the statement attributed to him, and the toast made by Hans Weegin is a direct quote of a toast made by Jedediah M. Grant, counselor to President Brigham Young.

In addition, fast days at that time were held on Thursdays, some women got around to washing their hair at least once every three or four years, tithing was paid in kind, bedbugs and lice were nearly as plentiful as beard-bugs, most polygamous husbands (who wore the beards that beard-bugs lived in) did their best to love all of their wives equally, the wives did their best to appreciate all the above arrangements, young people fell into and out of love, and soap and milk were made in the back yard rather than bought from the supermarket.

In short, times have changed. Even so, much of the story you are about to read is, for the most part, occasionally somewhat . . . well, you decide how much of it is true. And while you are deciding, we hope you have as much fun with it as we did.

1

The Mud Hen

The sound of a horse's hooves being sucked out of sticky mud drifted loudly across the late afternoon stillness. The rain had stopped, but still the air was heavy and threatening. The water had puddled in the bottom of the ditch where the bishop lay, and though it was mid-June, he found himself shivering uncontrollably.

Carefully he lifted his eyes to peer through the water-beaded grass which arched above him, trying to determine from one tiny patch of sky the complexion of the whole afternoon. Yet the grayness told him nothing, and he shivered again as a stream of icy water broke loose from the grass and cascaded onto the small of his unprotected back.

Again the sound of the horse came to his ears, this time closer, and desperately he pushed himself deeper into the mud, hoping and praying that he might remain undetected.

In his mind's eye the bishop could see vividly the man on the horse. Hebron Clawson, United States deputy marshal, would be sitting astride his ancient and ugly piebald gelding. He would have his slicker on, though it wouldn't be helping much, being so full of holes as it was. His drooping hat would be more droopy than ever, and his well-worn boots were probably filled with water from brushing through the nearly-ready-to-cut alfalfa. His foul-smelling cigar would of course be in his mouth, but more than likely it would be unlighted, simply because the rain collecting in his yellowed mustaches would have doused it.

Eternal minutes dragged along, and now the only sound coming to the bishop's ears was the constant but irregular dripping of water into the ditch. With effort he restrained an impulse to rise up for a careful look around. He might make it, but then he might not, too. He knew Deputy Clawson too well to take the chance. Far too well. True it was that he had a shoddy appearance, and true it was also that he cared little for the clothes he wore or the animals he rode, for these things were merely necessary tools to aid him in his job. But that job, the job Deputy Clawson did with untiring zeal each day of his life, was done with nothing at all that resembled shoddiness or carelessness.

For Hebron Clawson was a manhunter, or perhaps more appropriately he was a polygamist hunter, and he was very probably the best polyg-hunter in the entire territory of Utah. For that reason alone the bishop lay quietly in the bottom of the ditch.

Slowly the afternoon dripped along. The rain had started up again, a slow cold drizzle that did nothing but make everything just a bit more miserable than it had been before, and the bishop groaned inwardly at the thoughts of another two or three hours in the bottom of the ditch. His legs were now cramping from being still so long in the cold and wet, and it was agony trying to keep from rolling into a sitting position to knead his screaming muscles.

Off in town a dog barked, a lonesome kind of bark that was more a howling, and the man in the ditch thought of his own loneliness. True it was that he was the bishop, the supposed spiritual leader of the more than seven hundred citizens of his ward and community. And true it was also that he had three wives and fourteen children. Yet still he was lonely, with an aching kind of feeling within him that was impossible to explain or even to understand. He remembered well the day that John Taylor had discussed with him his new calling as bishop, and President Taylor had told him then that it would be the most lonely position he would ever have. How right the prophet had been! Always he was surrounded by people, and yet always he was lonely, for none of them could know of his feelings.

And add to that the polygamy problem. Three wives, piles of loving children, three comfortable homes, and here he was lying in the bottom of a miserable ditch with icy water his only loving companion. Where was the justice? Where was the—?

The nickering of the horse was so close and came with such suddenness that the bishop literally jumped, and as he cursed himself for dreaming he listened as the horse moved slowly in his direction. Silently he held his breath and pushed himself deeper into the mud, pressing even more tightly against the bank where he would be hidden by the overhanging grass. The sound of the horse was now directly above him. With half his mind he wondered how he had been discovered, while with the other half he wondered what he was going to do next. How would his family get along without him if he were in prison? How would the members of the ward—?

With a grunt the horse lunged across the ditch directly above the hidden bishop, and as it strained upward one of its hooves slipped on the mud bank and crashed to the bottom, striking the bishop a glancing blow to his shoulder.

The bishop, tensed anyway, let out an involuntary cry of pain as the hoof hit him. Instantly he realized his mistake and lunged to his feet to run.

The marshal's horse, unaware that anything but a ditch was beneath it, saw the man suddenly materialize at its side. In terror the animal rolled its eyes, laid back its ears, and lashed out with its hind feet in a vicious buck. In the next instant the gelding was fleeing headlong across the field, taking the marshal away from the apparition behind it as rapidly as possible.

Marshal Clawson, his reputation as the most able polyg-hunter in central Utah at stake, sawed the reins desperately against the neck of his fear-crazed horse. Over his shoulder he could see the most famous polygamist in Sanpete County slipping, skidding and sliding toward freedom. Blasted horse! If he hadn't needed it so badly the marshal would have made the animal into instant buzzard bait. Trouble was, it was a long walk home without his horse, and the marshal was not a walker. To his way of thinking, if a job couldn't be done from the back of a horse, then such job ought not to be done. So he held his drawn pistol in one hand, yanked on the reins with the other, and cursed his horse, the rain, and his luck.

The bishop, his lungs feeling as if they were about to burst, pushed himself as rapidly as possible across the alfalfa field toward town. He had no idea where he was going, except as far as possible from the deputy and from the muddy field. Problem was, if he went to one of his homes, that would be exactly where the deputy would look for him. If he went to anyone else's home there were two things to worry about. The first was that any individual who helped him would be aiding and abetting a known criminal—namely, him. The second thing was that he wasn't certain at all whom he could trust. After all, the reward money on his head was a sizeable thing. Fact is, more than once he'd wished there was a way that he could turn himself in just so he could collect it and pay a couple of his bills.

Marshals! Polygamy! Criminals! What a farce this whole thing was! The Constitution of the United States was supposed to grant him freedom of religion. Exercising that freedom, he had done as the leaders of the Church had commanded him and had taken more than one wife—three, to be exact—just like men in the Old Testament had done.

Then the government, bless its political and puritanical heart, had taken upon itself the role of tyrannical monitor of the Mormon religion. All kinds of measures and bills had been introduced and passed in Congress, and good Mormons who had always supported the principle of obedience not only to the law of God but also to the law of the land, suddenly found themselves outside the law and branded as criminals. It was a fine mess—as fine a mess as any he had ever seen—and the good bishop found himself right in the thick of it, playing the role of a fugitive rather than the role of husband, father, financier, and bishop like he ought to be doing. Why, if the marshals would let him alone, then—

The sound of the rapidly approaching horse forced his thoughts back to the precariousness of his present situation, and as he glanced over his shoulder he suddenly knew that he needn't worry about where he was going to flee. The question now, he knew, was no longer if he was going to be captured, but when, and how easy he should make it for the marshal. For that worthy had finally pulled his horse under control, turned it, and was even now fanning its rump with his reins, urging it to greater speed as he flew toward the bishop.

"Soderberg!" he yelled. "Hold up right there! I got this hogleg trained right on the middle of yer yellow back, and if ya don't rein up I'll blow a hole in ya so big your whole blasted ward can drive their buggies through it!"

The bishop, glancing back, could see the pistol all right, but he knew it wasn't aimed directly at anything, not the way that gelding was humping and sliding through the mud and the alfalfa. Still, if Clawson decided to shoot, he could get lucky, and the bishop didn't like the idea of going to the next costume ball dressed as a sieve. Some folks already claimed that he had holes in his head, and there was no point in going out of his way to prove them right.

The explosion of a .45 suddenly thundered in the bishop's ears, and in the same instant he felt a tug at his sleeve and heard the *whap* as the slug whipped past him.

"Oh no," he groaned. "Clawson is shooting for real! I reckon I'd best—"

Another explosion roared in his ears, much closer, though again it was a miss, and he looked over his shoulder just in time to see the marshal's ugly gelding, flecked with mud and foam, come thundering down upon him. The bishop tried to dodge back, to get out of the way, but his feet were as much out of control as were those of the horse, and in an instant he was knocked sprawling into the mud and the alfalfa.

Deputy Clawson, so close to his prey, now suddenly found himself being carried once more in the wrong direction. Hauling on the reins, he looked back in time to see the bishop struggle to his feet, wipe the mud from his face, and stagger off in another direction.

"Confounded beast!" Clawson shouted, whipping his animal once more with his reins. "Git on around there! Most awkward blamed cayuse I ever been astride of. Come nightfall, you mangy critter, and you'll be buzzard meat for sure.

"Soderberg, blast yer Mormon hide! Hold up there or you'll be the deadest dang bishop in all of Sanpete County. Thunderation if I ever saw anybody with as much run in 'em as you've got. Yer yellow streak must be three-quarters of a mile wide just on yer shoulders, and I reckon it get wider as it goes down. All gurgle and no guts! That's what I said before, and that's what I say now.

"Git up, horse! Git them feet under you and git going! Blasted critter's as awkward as a blind bear in a bramble patch. Thunderation, Soderberg, hold up there, I say!''

Bishop Soderberg, cold, wet, tired, and very, very sore, glanced back to see Deputy Clawson on his piebald gelding barreling down on him once again. And suddenly, for the first time since he had been made bishop, the proverbial patience that was supposed to be one of his never-ending virtues climbed on its own pony and galloped off, leaving the bishop alone with his temper and Deputy Clawson.

Now it must be understood that Bishop Jons Soderberg was not a small man, not in the size of his family, not in dreams, not in acquisitions, and certainly not in physical bulk. Fact is, folks in town liked to say that he was big enough to hunt bear with a switch, and likely they weren't far wrong. Of a weekend he'd go to church, conduct the meetings, and then race the young boys home, carrying a cedar post for a handicap. Ofttimes the older sisters would shake their heads in disgust at such goings on, but that didn't slow the bishop down, at least not so's a body would notice. Why, one Sunday he even packed his two counselors home, one sitting astride each of his shoulders, and those two holding that cedar post above his head. So when it is said that if he put his heart to moving something, it usually moved, that ought to be accepted as known fact.

The other thing that ought to be understood is that Bishop Soderberg was by nature a peaceable man, not too easily riled. His calling as the bishop made him even more inclined toward peace, and so despite his size he was known as one who walked away from fighting. In fact, if the truth be known, there were some who were not even that kind. They simply called him a flat-out coward. Marshal Clawson was one of those, and he sincerely believed that the bishop was indeed that—a coward, pure and simple.

That was why, when the bishop skidded to a halt and turned to face the deputy, warning bells did not go off in the deputy's mind. And that was a shame, too, for up to this point the only mud the United States deputy marshal had on him was what his horse had splattered on his legs.

And so now Deputy Clawson grinned, for there was the polygamist bishop, Jons Soderberg, standing there waiting for him, willing to surrender and further the legend the marshal knew was building in the territory about himself. Only again his blasted horse was moving too fast to stop when it was supposed to, and it was still humping along at a pretty good clip when it reached the fugitive. That was when Marshal Clawson first saw the look of anger and determination showing beneath the mud on the bishop's face. Then it was that the warning bells rang, but by then it was way too late for warnings to do any good—any good at all.

For the bishop, suddenly and unexpectedly, reached out and took hold of the reins of the still-moving piebald on which rode the hapless marshal. With a mighty heave the bishop hauled down on those reins, pulling the gelding's head down almost to the ground. That, of course, stopped the front end of that horse from going anywhere. Trouble was, the hind end of the animal was still set on traveling, and it continued to do so, straight up into the air and on over the top of its buried head.

"Anti-I-over!" shouted Bishop Soderberg as the piebald completed its flip with an awkward and heavy *kersplatt* into the mud of the alfalfa field.

"Eeeeyyyyiiiii!" shouted Deputy Clawson, who suddenly had all options but one removed from his bag of choices. Whereas a moment before he had been about to arrest the most wanted polyg in the county, he now found himself airborne. He flailed his arms and his legs in a vain attempt to lengthen his flight or soften his landing, not caring very much which. Nothing worked, however, and with a *kersploosh* he did a belly-flop in the mud, where he slid to a halt some twenty feet from his still-struggling horse.

For a few seconds he fought to regain his breath. When it returned he started searching for his dignity, which had also been knocked from him. Then, just as he was getting to his feet, a voice behind and above him brought him to a dead stop.

"Deputy Clawson," the bishop said quietly, "reckon if I were you I'd hold it right there. One false move and I'll blow a hole in you so big my whole ward will be able to drive their buggies through it."

Slowly the marshal turned to look, and he felt something within him shrivel up and die when he saw Bishop Soderberg perched on top of his mud-covered horse with the marshal's gun in his hand and a grin on his face.

"Deputy," he continued, "seems to me I ought to do something about terminating this relationship of ours. We just can't go on meeting like this. I mean, what'll folks say and all?"

Slowly then the bishop lifted up the pistol until it was trained on the marshal.

"Soderberg, no! Don't shoot! I wasn't going to kill you! I swear it! I never did aim to hit you! Only scare you into stopping, that was all I wanted, that was all I. . . ."

The bishop, as though he heard nothing of the deputy's wailings, continued to sight along the barrel of the pistol.

"Yep, just like I thought. The barrel on this weapon is bent, and the whole thing is covered with mud and dirt. Deputy, you ought to be ashamed, representing the U. S. government with a weapon in such deplorable condition as this one is. Why, I'm of a mind to report you to Marshal Dyer in Salt Lake City for carelessness.

"Of course, I'm a mite careless myself, being caught out here on a day like this without a slicker or a horse. Still, that is no one's fault but my own, as I left my home in much haste, fearing a real bad man was after me. Why, I reckon we can both see what a foolish notion that one was. So I've been careless, and you've been careless, and that seems to pretty much even up the score. Don't you think?

"Now, deputy, we could sit here jawing all day, and I don't mean to be rude, but it seems to me I've enjoyed about all of your hospitality I can stand, at least for today. With your leave, then, I'll be on my way. And deputy, I hope we'll meet again. I surely do. The next time we meet I won't have to borrow your horse. No, sir, I'll have one of my own then, a mover that will sail away from such company as you like a bird from a tree. Until then, adios.''

"Soderberg!" the deputy shouted, suddenly angry, "I'll have you for horse stealing, horse stealing and resisting arrest and weapon stealing and insulting a U. S. officer and—and—''

"Temper, my good marshal, temper. Take a moment and clean the mud out of your ears. I'm borrowing, not stealing. Didn't you hear me? Why, what would a man like me want with a bent-up pistol and an ugly, broken-down, sway-backed cayuse like this one? Merciful heavens! Except for this once, I'd not be caught dead on such a critter. No, sir, Brother Marshal, I'm only borrowing. Later on today you'll find this critter tied to the gate by the cemetery north of town. You'll also find this worthless pistol tied to the saddle. And, marshal, don't tarry too long at the cemetery. There's some that say those old polygamists buried in there are restless of a night and prowl around looking for nice juicy marshals.

"Now, once again, adios. It sure is a beautiful afternoon for a walk, don't you think? See you around, Brother Marshal!''

Angrily Deputy Clawson stalked through the mud and the rain and the alfalfa, his eyes riveted on the retreating back of the bishop. Never, never in his whole life had he been so humiliated, so—so—

"Blast!" he swore as he kicked viciously at a clump of alfalfa. "I'll get that man! I'll arrest him if it's the last arrest I ever make!''

2

The Eighteen Hundred
Dollar Plug

I think that if Pa had known a little more about horses, there wouldn't have been any problems. Trouble was, Pa was only an expert in maybe three things, those being the Church, making money, and getting married, and not necessarily in that order. Not that I'm against any of them, of course, but that day Pa surely could have used a little more savvy about horses. If he had, what I'm about to relate would probably never have happened. But it did, and here is how.

It had been about ten days since Pa had come home from the field all muddied up and mounted on Deputy Clawson's gelding, and about all he'd talked about since then, at least while I was around, was finding a horse that would be faster and stronger than any other horse in the territory. He was not, he declared over and over, about to lie freezing in another ditch when a fine horse could be carrying him off to safety. So every day Pa was out hunting for horses and dickering on them, which left his wives and us children at home doing our best to hold things together.

This day Ma had pulled me out of bed right early so I could get over to Ammon Hanson's and get a big old wart charmed off my hand. I got there, and he took a hunk of raw bacon and rubbed the wart like crazy, wiped it all off with an old dishrag, and then took the dishrag and buried it somewhere out in his orchard. I don't know how it worked, but it did. I'd had two of them charmed off before, so I didn't doubt for a minute that it would work. It took a week or two, of course, but the warts always went. Besides, it was painless, and since I'm allergic to pain I didn't mind his treatment at all.

When I got home Ma had rounded up my half-brothers Jim and Lyman, two boys belonging to Pa's first wife, Aunt Polly, and Johnny, who was the only son in town belonging to Victoria, Pa's second wife. I could tell that today was going to be as exciting as the rest of them, for Pa had left word for us to get down to the bishops' storehouse to help Elinor, one of my half-sisters, with another day's work on the tithing. Now I don't mind work if it is done with moderation, but it always seemed easier for Pa, as bishop, to get work out of us than to make a work call from the pulpit. Today was even worse than most, though, because we had ninety-six tithing chickens to butcher. Imagine that! I never could understand why some folks couldn't kill and clean their own tithing before they brought it in.

Well, anyway, we had just dumped the first bucket of scalding water, having plucked seventeen of those foul-smelling fowls, when we heard the most gosh-awful thunder of hooves pounding up the lane. It sounded like Pa was on the run again, except that Pa didn't have a horse that sounded like that. Dropping the axe, I found myself, as always, hobbling a step behind the others as thcy vaulted the woodpile and headed up through the potato patch. That was risky, since Ma had a switch handy for anyone, man or beast, caught running through the ward's "needy garden." Nonetheless we made it, and I was just running around the side of the shed, limping full-tilt, when both horse and rider jerked to a stop practically right on top of me. I stumbled back out of the way, the horse reared in fright, and Pa, yelling at me to watch what I was doing, grabbed leather and clung to that horse with all his might. Again it was obvious that Pa was not a horseman.

After a minute or so Jim got hold of the bridle and calmed the horse, and then Pa lit into me, giving me the worst tongue-lashing I'd had in years. And I reckon maybe I deserved it, too, for I surely did get in the way of Pa and his new horse.

For that is what it turned out to be. After Pa got through with me he turned to Ma, and with the widest grin on his face I'd seen since he'd saved old Hepsi, our cow, from the mud mire, he said, "Hattie, what do you think of my horse?"

Ma didn't answer, not at first. She just stood there staring, along with the rest of us, at Pa sitting on top of the biggest doggonedest horse any of us had ever seen.

"Gosh," I gasped. "Whose cayuse is that, Pa?"

Without even answering me, Pa swung out of the saddle quicker than chain lightning with a link snapped, picked up Ma, and started twirling her around like they were in the middle of a ball somewhere.

"Well, Hattie," he grinned, "I finally got it. Slickest horse trading I ever did. Why, those gents were sure square shooters, and by golly, they weren't even Saints. Isn't he a beaut! Pure-blooded registered Belgian stallion, not a mark on him, and eighteen hands high if he's an inch!"

"But, Pa," I shouted, forgetting again who I was in relation to who he was, "he's a plug! That ain't no riding horse! Why, look at those feet. They're big enough to plug badger holes and stomp out grizzlies!"

"Hyrum," Pa said quietlike, turning on me again, "curb your tongue. You seem to have forgotten who you are talking to. Just because you are nearly full-grown, that does not give you the right to rattle your tongue at your father.

"Now, I'll grant you that he is big, but I guarantee that this horse will outrun any other four-legged, saddle-packing critter in Sanpete County. Why, I've just come from Victoria's home, and before that I came up from Ephraim. And, Hyrum, you and your smart tongue might be interested in knowing that I stopped in at our dairy, and who should be there but Deputy Clawson, looking for yours truly."

"Jons?" Ma asked anxiously.

"It's all right, Hattie. Don't worry. Clawson got the drop on me, all right. But he didn't tie my hands. He just took my reins, held his pistol on me, and ordered me to ride. So I did, and as soon as he was relaxed I reached up, slipped the bridle off of old Ingersol here, and the two of us took off. Well, you never saw such a surprised marshal. I hit that front gate, the one I rigged with the trick weighted latch, and we sailed through it and were off before Clawson even realized that we were gone. By the time he figured the gate out and got through it himself, Ingersol and I were into the trees on the south end of Cedar Hill, two miles away from him and gaining.

"A plug this horse may be, Hyrum. But I'll tell you this, he is the fastest plug I've ever had the pleasure of riding. In five miles I outran Deputy Clawson by nearly three of them. Son, that is riding. In fact, I am convinced that there isn't a horse in the county that this animal couldn't daylight. And that includes those two white mares of Mungus Sorenson's. Yes, sir, this is one fine animal."

By now we were even more amazed, and so we just stood there slack-jawed while Pa showed off the points of that high-quality hunk of horseflesh to Ma.

Thing was, we got so wrapped up in Pa's new horse that we didn't hear anyone approaching until the springs creaked in a buckboard behind us. Then we turned to see Mungus Sorenson jumping down.

Now, Mungus was probably the last man I would have expected to see at the storehouse. He was what we called a Jack-Mormon, and he had been since he stormed out of the meetinghouse the day Pa was made bishop. Pa says it was tough on Mungus to watch an outsider be made bishop, for he was sort of aspiring to the position himself. When the authorities in Mt. Pleasant asked Pa to move up from Moroni to lead the Aspen Wells Saints, it was just too much for him. Mungus had spread the word that he would never again set foot on Church property until Pa was released. That was why it was so surprising to see Mungus at the storehouse. And his gloating look had me right puzzled.

"Well, bishop," he grinned, "who in tarnation is so poor that they have to pay tithing with a worn-out, half-dead piece of horseflesh like that?"

We all froze, knowing first-hand of Pa's temper, which was slow to boil but scary when it did. Ma even put her hand on Pa's arm, though as it turned out she didn't need to. Pa simply turned his back on Mungus and began digging out the horse's hooves with his pocket knife.

"Mungus," he inquired, finally looking up, "how have you been?"

"It isn't me that we ought to be worried about, bishop. No, sirree, it surely isn't. Your wife Victoria was just up to the Co-op, and she told us right proudly that you had paid eighteen hundred dollars cash for that nag. Now, bishop, that worries me. In fact, it worries me a lot. I worry because no one in his right mind would ever pay that much for a plug. Only you did, and that troubles me, for I see all these good folks here in Aspen Wells allowing themselves to be led by such a man. And bishop, that brings me to my second concern. Eighteen hundred dollars cash! I wonder where you got that much money? I wonder if we don't need an audit of the tithing office?

"So anyway, I just stopped by to see this horse for myself. I had to find out if what your wife said was true, or if she was fabricating somewhat, like her husband is prone to do."

I don't know about my brothers, but I was so shocked by what Mungus had said and implied that I simply held my breath, knowing that Pa was about to clean his meathouse. Ma looked like she had just been slugged, but when she spoke I was surprised at what had upset her.

"Jons," she gasped, "is that true? You couldn't have paid that much for a horse! Not when. . . ."

Without even so much as looking at Ma or at the rest of us, Pa slowly rose to his feet and walked over to where Mungus was standing. It had suddenly grown so quiet that I could hear a bee buzzing somewhere nearby, and the birds in the willows down by the creek sounded closer than they ever had before. I was even aware of a bead of sweat that was trickling down my spine.

Pa stood for a moment, gazing intently into Mungus's face, and then very calmly he spoke.

"Mungus," he said, nearly whispering, "you listen, and you listen hard. Don't you ever call one of my wives a liar again! Do you hear? If you have something to say about me, then drag up your stock and run it around the corral a few times so we can see how the brand lies. But don't you ever malign one of my family again! Now kindly climb back up into that wagon of yours and rattle your hocks on out of here, before I lose my temper and read you from the book.''

''Why, yes sir, bishop,'' Mungus grinned. ''Anything you say, bishop.''

With that he wheeled around, leaped into his rig, and picked up his reins.

''Say, bishop,'' he yelled as his team of matching white mares started to turn, ''Victoria said you bought that nag because it was fast. You wouldn't care to make a little wager on that, would you? I mean, if it is as fast as your wife said it is, I'd like to see it run.''

Without answering, Pa took Ma's arm and walked toward the storehouse, his face a study in barely controlled anger. With that, my brothers and I hightailed it back to the woodpile and our chickens. We knew Pa would have sent us back anyway, and right then we would have fought mountain lions rather than incur Pa's wrath. Fact is, I was amazed that Mungus had gotten off so easily.

One thing for sure, Pa's new horse had surely muddied the water in the puddle called Aspen Wells. How much, though, I wouldn't learn until later that night.

3

The Eighteen Hundred
Dollar Kiss

It was hard to believe how quickly word spread about Pa and his new horse. By the time conjoint session for the young people started that evening, the news of his purchase was the main topic of conversation. He, and by implication all of his family, were having their sanity questioned. And that is saying it mildly.

Now, I'm kind of used to talk such as that, having a crippled foot and all, so I have learned to pay it no mind when folks start laughing at me. I mean, if a fellow gets all het up every time some person starts poking fun at him, then he's going to spend his whole life being angry. For a time I went that route, but it didn't take too long for me to see that I wasn't going anywhere. That was when I finally made up my mind that I had too many more important things to do to. I wasn't going to waste my life being angry all the time.

So that night when the fellows started making fun of Pa and the rest of us, I just naturally pulled in my horns and started to walk off. Trouble was, Jim and Lyman had never learned how to do that, and Jim especially is one of those fellows who won't be pushed for sour apples.

20

I've heard some folks say Jim is mean, and it is true that he has occasionally hung kids by their heels in picket fences, leaving them there to rot when they wouldn't let up on him. But mean? No, mostly he just likes to tease. Still, he's rolling thunder when he gets riled. That I will admit.

So that night when Pete Livingston and Curly Sorenson, Mungus's boy, started crowding us, why, old Jim just wouldn't crowd. Pete and Curly started calling us "plugs" when they first saw us coming up the street, and by the time we got up to them there must have been about twenty fellows chanting all kinds of unpleasantries in our direction.

Now to me that seemed like quite a crowd, but Lyman and Jim just saw them as a challenge, as though the odds were about even. Why, one day when three Feds were hassling Aunt Polly and giving her grief, Jim took Pa's pistol and got the drop on them. He then told them to get off the property or he'd whup them all, one at a time or all at once, and it didn't much matter to him which. Well, those marshals knew he was just a boy, but they took one good look at the man-sized pistol he was holding, and they left, every last one of them. Nope, Jim didn't have a single fear-bone in his body, nor Lyman either, for that matter, though he was more quiet about it. In fact, I suspect that if it had been Lyman who got the drop on the Feds, he wouldn't have offered to fight them, he would have just waded in and done it, and then maybe talked about it afterwards. Both my brothers take after Pa where all this is concerned, though Pa did a whole lot of settling down when they called him to Aspen Wells to be the bishop.

Pa did tell us that we ought to avoid fighting as much as possible. But if we were going to fight, he said, we might as well fight to win. He also told us most fights were won with the first punch, and that we ought to land the first one good and hard, the way General Moroni did it in the Book of Mormon. So Jim and Lyman, taking Pa's advice to heart, marched up to Pete and Curly, who were joking and elbowing each other, having a right good time poking fun at Pa, his horse, and all the rest of us. We were outnumbered, they knew it, and they were all set on having a wonderful time giving us a little verbal abuse.

"Hi, ya, Petey-boy," was all Jim said, and he was smiling when he said it, a nice easy kind of smile that was as innocent as a newborn babe. Pete stood there kind of surprised, taken back by the quietness of it all, and I reckon he was still trying to understand why Jim wasn't mad when his nose got spread all over his face. At the same moment, Lyman let Curly have a stiff one in the wind section; Curly doubled over, and then Lyman introduced Curly's face to his kneecap.

Well, things got pretty exciting then, with those two boys, like Samson among the Philistines, smiting their brethren hip and thigh, fist and foot, and head and knee as well.

Right off I could see that while those two heathen brothers of mine were having the time of their lives, the odds were not exactly in their favor, and they maybe could do with a little help. So, making myself as inconspicuous as I could, I limped up behind Hank Forest, who was just getting set to throw himself on Lyman's back. Then I lifted up that heavy-handled cane Pa had given me for Christmas and I began pounding some whole new thoughts into Hank's mind. The next fellow I made an impression on was Spike Mills, and then the three of us, my brothers and I, were back to back and earnestly practicing the laying on of hands.

Well, for the next few minutes we had more ups and downs than a charging caterpillar, and by the time Pa's counselor, Ollie Olsen, came out and pulled what was left of those fellers off from us, we were all chomping dust and picking gravel out of our knuckles.

I don't recall the last time I hurt so bad, and I don't remember the last time I felt so good, either. All three of us—Jim, Lyman, and I—we got to our feet and stood there together, breathing hard, trying to spit out the salty taste of blood and sweat, and, in general, swelling our chests.

Ollie then proceeded to yell at us, I think for fighting, though the way it came out it sounded like he was angry simply because we were the bishop's sons.

When he'd finished, Jim grinned at him, picked up my hat and handed it to me, and then the three of us filed through that crowd of bloody faces and—

And that was when I first noticed Ida Mae. She wasn't doing anything, just standing there staring, her eyes bigger than anything I'd ever seen.

Now I reckon I'd better say a little about Ida Mae. She was Mungus Sorenson's daughter, Curly's little sister, and she was about the cutest little lady I'd ever seen, a pure grade A, blue ribbon girl. Fact is, if the truth were known, I'd had a case on her ever since I first noticed that she was a female, and that had been maybe three full weeks, give or take a day. I didn't know exactly where she lived, never having had the opportunity or courage to find out, but I'd heard she and Mungus and Curly lived on some two-by-twice rawhide outfit somewhere south of town.

So there was Ida Mae, staring at the fellows who had just been feeding her brother a supper of knuckle sandwiches, and suddenly I was sick inside. I'd never spoken to her, never even looked at her when she was looking back, always admiring her from afar, so to speak. And now I realized that all my dreams, all my hopes, all my plans, had been drowned in the blood and sweat of a fistfight. Hang it all, I—

Without warning, something heavy smashed into my skull. I saw Ida Mae, and it looked like she was screaming. Then the ground was coming up at me, and the next thing I knew it was all dark and quiet, my head was hurting like blue blazes, and someone right close by was crying.

With an effort I opened one eye, just enough to see a few stars above the roof of the meetinghouse. Then someone leaned over me, blocking out the stars, and I felt a cool damp cloth wiping my face. Then a hand, all soft and warm, pressed gently against my cheek and my chin, and of a sudden I knew what was happening. Some girl critter had hold of me.

With a yelp of fear I lunged up, and in the instant before dizziness got the best of me I saw the face of Ida Mae, all anxious and worried as she reached out to steady me.

Then I was on the ground again and it was funny how I knew everything that was going on but was unable to do anything about it.

23

Ida Mae was kneeling in the dirt beside me and she was holding my head against her, and the last time any female had done that it had been Ma. Thing was, somehow it surely felt different this time. And I couldn't decide whether I liked it or not.

Suddenly that blasted fear of girls seized me again, and I shoved her hands away and pulled myself once more to my feet.

"Say!" I shouted, sounding much louder than I had intended. "Where are they?"

"Who?" she replied quietly.

"Jim and Lyman is who. And how come I'm here alone with you?"

"That's right," she said thoughtfully. "You wouldn't know, would you? Your brothers are somewhere chasing that dumb brother of mine. When Curly hit you over the head Jim and Lyman lit out after him like hounds after a rabbit. You'd best get inside now and set yourself down. No fooling, you look worse than third-day porridge."

Well, if she wasn't flattering at least she was honest, and to tell the truth I didn't feel much better than I apparently looked. So I made my way into the meetinghouse and sat there hurting and dreaming for the rest of the meeting. Golly, did my head hurt! I felt worse than a calf with the slobbers. On the other hand, though, wasn't that Ida Mae something! Maybe that big old plug of Pa's was worth eighteen hundred smackers after all.

Lyman and Jim and the other fellows came in toward the end of the meeting, and Jim handed me back my cane. Then the three of us sat there together and I'll tell a man I was proud as punch, sitting next to those two. We did miss Johnny, who was out at the herd, and Ernest, who was learning to irrigate. Both of them had missed all the fun. Still, it was great being part of a big close family like ours was. Folks can say what they want about polygamy—but me, I like big families.

When the meeting ended, all the young people started filing out through the back door, girls first. It was like a mass movement that I was swept up in, following those girls just like I knew what I was doing. And to tell the truth, I was getting caught up in the excitement as much as the other fellows. Now, like I said, I'd only known girls were alive for about three weeks, and of all the girls in my ward only Ida Mae had taken my fancy. And in that three weeks I'd either been irrigating or working down at the dairy, so this was my first conjoint session, so to speak, where I was aware of the girls. It was fun and it was scary all at the same time.

Once outside, we all stood around shoving each other and generally acting foolish. I was straining my neck trying to locate Ida Mae when some lunkhead pushed me into a whole crowd of girls. They started giggling and I staggered back, and then not knowing what to say I just stood there with my hands in my pockets, feeling the red creep up my neck and across my face. Boy, was I ever glad it was dark!

Well, then all of us, boys and girls, stood around and made funnies, and Joe Spinner did some fancy walking along the top of Anderson's fence. And then suddenly, as if by some prearranged signal, Joe jumped off the fence and the whole crowd followed him off down the street.

I didn't know what to do, so I ended up doing nothing except just standing there, feeling dumb. Lyman saw me, though, and shouted, "Hey, Hy, come on! Don't just stand there like a bump on a stump. Let's go!"

At that, everyone turned to stare, and I heard a couple of girls giggle, so with burning ears I kicked myself where a fellow ought to be kicked occasionally and caught up. My hands were still in my pockets, and my cane was tucked tightly under my arm where I hoped no one could see it.

I didn't know where we were going at all, but I couldn't think of a good way to ask without looking more foolish than I already did. So I just kept walking, figuring that it would all come out in the wash.

After walking for what seemed like forever (though it was only a block or so), I was shoved into Jim. So I grabbed his arm and asked him where we were going.

"We're walking the girls home, dummy. Wheredidya think?"

Okay, so I wouldn't ask Jim any more questions that night. Still, now I knew, and I supposed it sounded safe enough. I mean, it was dark, and I could remain anonymous in the crowd. No one would notice me, so what did I care if we walked the girls home or not? It couldn't take too long, so there still should be plenty of time to milk Hepsi when I got home.

Then I happened to glance to the side just as two fellows and two girls peeled off from the group and turned down a side street together. I was still wondering at that when Lyman broke off from the crowd and walked away with that Hanson girl, and the way he was acting I could tell he was lady-broke for sure. And now I was getting nervous! Something was happening, and whatever it was, it was getting out of hand!

In the next three blocks the boys and girls peeled off at regular intervals, and it wasn't too long before I realized two things—no, three things. The first was that not only Lyman but Jim too was gone, leaving me alone. Well, not alone, exactly. My second realization was that there were only six of us left. And that brought me to my third realization, the most scary one of all.

I was walking beside Ida Mae Sorenson!

It was too dark to see her very well, but I could tell that up close she was a little shorter than me, and that she had her hair done up in a bun, neither of which I'd noticed earlier. She was walking along with her hands held in front of her, her arms down straight and held tightly against her dress.

And me? I had my own hands as far down in my pockets as they would possibly go. We were awfully close together, so carefully, trying not to draw her attention, I inched away from her two or three feet. That flower water she had on was simply overpowering.

Well, I was just trying to sort out the butterflies when another couple took off for another front door and there were only four of us left. The other two were talking and giggling a little, but you can bet I wasn't. I was as silent as a graveyard at midnight, and a whole lot more nervous. For the life of me I couldn't understand how I had ever gotten into this mess. Here I was, alone, walking along a dirt road in the dark with a girl I had never so much as spoken to until that night. That was scary.

But what was even more scary was the fact that we were coming to the edge of town and I didn't even know where she lived. I could have shot myself for being so dumb. But then we went past some old poplar trees and I could see that there was only one house left.

What a relief! We were almost there. Sensing my ordeal to be about over, I turned into the path, only to stumble over Dave Connaly, who had just turned toward the gate with the Pritchett girl. Now what?

Just then the silence broke, and Ida Mae softly asked, "Where are you going, Hyrum?"

Hyrum? Why, she actually said my name! My heart did a couple of flip-flops as I squeaked, "In here. This is where you live, ain't it?"

"Isn't," she corrected. "And no, it isn't. This is where Kathy Pritchett lives."

Well, I tell you, I was dumbfounded. This was the last house. Anybody could see that. If she didn't live here, then where in blue blazes *did* she live?

She was walking on now, quite slowly, swishing her skirt back and forth as she walked, so desperately I clambered to catch up with her. By now Pa's horse and my fistfight had taken leave from my mind, and I was thinking some whole new thoughts. Something was happening way down deep inside me, something I'd started to feel after the fight, but which I was now feeling a whole lot. It is hard to describe that feeling, but it was like a cross between being sick and being in heaven, or something like that, anyway.

Anyway, I had to know where Ida Mae lived, and the only way I could think of finding out was to ask her. So I swallowed a couple of times, cleared my throat real quietly so it wouldn't squeak, and then I blurted, "All right, if you don't live there, then where do you live?"

And hang it all, despite my throat clearing I still croaked. I couldn't believe how much I sounded like a frog, especially when it was important that I not sound that way. I tell you, I was fast becoming a mental wreck, and I didn't know what to do about it.

Somehow, though, I found the courage to look over at her, and when I did I immediately wished that I hadn't. Why, she was *smiling* at me! Well, I gulped a couple of times, looked around for a rock to kick, and pushed my hands even deeper into my pockets.

Why was she looking at me, and why was she smiling at me? For crying out loud, was I supposed to look back at her and smile myself? There was no way on earth that I could do that.

"Do you see that light up there?" she suddenly whispered, breaking the agonizing silence. "Well, that light is in our window."

I squinted desperately into the darkness, trying to see the light. Normally I had pretty good vision, but still it was a minute or so before I saw, dimly and barely visible, on top of a mountain about a hundred miles away, a tiny flicker of light.

"You mean that light way out there?"

"Uh-huh. That's where I live."

As she spoke, I noticed for the first time that her voice was sounding sticky, like syrup or molasses or something. So cautiously I moved another foot or so away from her.

"Do you walk that far all the time?" I squeaked, not knowing what else to say.

"Only when I want to," she said. And now she smiled at me again, that same sticky smile. "Hyrum, I wanted to tonight."

Well, now, what in tarnation does a feller say to that? "Me, too"? Not on your life you don't. Not if your name is Hyrum. And mine was. I moved even further toward the ditch, suddenly noticing that she had somehow inched closer to me.

Right then my stomach was tied up in a million knots, I was so full of conflicting emotions. But one thing was for sure: Ida Mae would never know how I was feeling. Just because I liked her was no reason for her to know it. It was a lot more comfortable liking her from a distance. Still, I had to talk to her about something.

At that moment, something that Pa always said popped into my mind.

"Boys," he said, "if you ever lack for confabulation, just ask someone about the Bible."

Well, it was worth a try, so I up and did it. I asked her, I mean.

"Have you ever took to reading the Holy Word?" I inquired, my voice squeaking again.

"Taken, Hyrum, taken. And yes, Father occasionally reads to Curly and me at breakfast. But I've never actually read it myself. Do you read it, Hyrum?"

28

Well, I'll be . . . ! Here I was, having my first ever real talk with a girl, and suddenly I felt a strange new confidence.

"Why, sure," I blurted. "Pa has us learn a new verse every week. Says it will be good for us if he ever feels to call us into the mission field."

"Oh, can you quote scripture? I think men who can quote scripture are so wonderful! Hyrum, quote me a scripture, please."

I hesitated, and right off she opened her eyes wide and started imploring me again. But I couldn't. Blast! What a time to go blank. And even worse, I got so busy trying to remember some scripture that I didn't even notice that she was working herself toward me again. At least, I didn't notice until she was almost to me. But then, with a bit of fast thinking, I reached down, grabbed a rock, and took a couple of quick steps to throw it. Thus I got away from her again.

And just as I did so, the perfect scripture popped into my mind. It was one Lyman had taught me while we were at the sheep herd the summer before.

"Here's your scripture," I said. "Are you ready for it?"

"Oh, yes," she breathed, and suddenly I got the shivers. This girl was the most unpredictable creature I had ever laid eyes on.

"Okay, but remember, when someone learns a scripture, he's bound to do what it says. No matter what. Do you still want to hear it?"

"Uh-huh."

"All right, here it is. It's found in St. John, chapter 20, verse 17. It reads, 'He saith unto her, touch me not.' That's all I can remember."

Well, she got a funny look on her face, but it only lasted for a minute or so before the moon ducked behind a cloud, and that sudden things were back to normal. We walked in silence for a few yards, and then she spoke again.

"Hyrum, you do know my name, don't you?"

"Oh, er . . . yes . . . it's Ida, isn't it?"

"Ida Mae, Hyrum. But you can call me Ida if you'd like. From you, maybe I'd like that better."

"Oh," I choked. What was happening? Why all the special treatment? Was I imagining things? Did she maybe like me, or what?

Silence again. Silence and darkness.

"Hyrum?"

"Uh . . . yeah?"

"I'm really sorry about Curly hurting you like he did. He had no call to do that. Just because your father's gone and bought an old plug for a riding horse gives Curly no right to—"

"Now hold up right there, Ida Mae. Ingersol might be big, but Pa says he's fast, too. Mighty fast. He ain't no plug!"

"Isn't," she corrected. "Isn't any plug."

"Yeah," I breathed, relieved that she had come around so quickly to my way of thinking. "That's what I said. No marshal will ever catch him now."

"Do the marshals bother him a lot?"

"Well, I should smile they do. Whenever Pa's at home, one of us has to go act as lookout for their dust. He can't hardly rest, and he can't ever get anything done because he always has to move around. I'd say they bother him a whole lot."

She didn't say anything then, so for a month or two we walked along in uncomfortable silence, her swishing her skirts back and forth and me limping along beside her doing my best to act natural. That was tough, though, for somehow that girl surely addled my think-box. Ma says that I'm right smart, but for all I'm supposed to know I couldn't think of a single thing to say.

Something else that was bothering me was . . . well, me. From all appearances this girl acted as though she liked me, and that was a strange thing to consider. I mean, I've already mentioned my bad foot, but besides that, I'm skinnier than a peeled-off bean pole, and I heard Ma telling Pa one day that my teeth hadn't set straight. In other words, I was ugly. I knew it, everyone else knew it, and I honestly didn't know what I could do about it. Of course, being ugly didn't matter so much when I was around my brothers, for they had about the same problems I did, and each of them, in his own way, was ugly too. In fact, we often talked about that, trying to come up with ways of building our muscles and doing other things to improve our almost impossible looks.

Neither did being ugly matter too much when we were around our sisters, because sisters love brothers anyway, and never give much notice to the way they look. That is, they don't unless a brother happens to get real dirty or wear the wrong color of socks or something to meeting. And mothers? Well, you've heard the expression that some fellow has a face only his mother could love? Somebody said that for a good reason, and that was because it was occasionally true, myself being one prime example, as I have mentioned.

So add this all up and you can understand why I was having trouble understanding why Ida Mae seemed to be enjoying my company so much. There were just too many other fellows, good-looking ones, like Joe Spinner for instance, who could set a girl's heart to thumping.

So I was worrying that over in my mind when, without warning, Ida Mae sneaked up beside me and slipped her hand through my arm. I was so startled by the suddenness of the attack that I jumped at least thirty feet into the air. Yet somehow she held on and managed to look unruffled about it all.

I tell you, there isn't anything in the world that will discombobulate a fellow faster than a pretty girl. And that is especially true if he hasn't gotten at least a little used to the idea that he is near one. I was so nervous that I was like a piece of walking oak, but Ida Mae didn't even seem to notice. She just walked along slowly beside me, swishing her skirts back and forth like she was in the May Day parade.

"Hyrum?"

"Huh?"

"Don't you think the stars are pretty tonight?"

The stars! Good grief! Who had time to think about stars? I was still trying to think of some way to escape, or at least say something funny. It was obvious that she had not gotten the drift of Lyman's scripture.

"Yeah, I guess they are," I replied at last. "They look cold, though."

"Cold? Oh, Hyrum, I don't think so! To me they look warm, full of love, full of life. To me they are so . . . so . . . romantic."

Romantic? I tell you, she'd caught me completely off guard. I didn't know where this conversation was going, but I hoped it took longer for it to get there than it did for us to reach her front gate.

Trouble was, that light on her porch looked farther away than ever, and I was beginning to wonder if we were ever going to make it.

"Hyrum?"

Oh, no! What did she want now? That tone she had in her voice was one I'd heard before. Ma used it when she wanted Pa to do something that he found particularly disagreeable, but which he always seemed to end up doing. Hearing her use it on me, though, was about enough to scare the bejeebies out of me!

"Hyrum?"

"Huh?"

"Hyrum, may I ask you a question?" she asked coyly, and I felt the shivers start up my spine. I heard once that if you felt that, it meant someone was stepping on your grave. Well, I could believe it. This whole experience was scaring me to death.

"Well, may I?"

"Er, I don't know," I said lamely, knowing she was coyoting around the rim of something I wouldn't like, but not knowing what I could do about it. She looked at me then, with those big eyes of hers, and suddenly I felt bad. I mean, I felt somehow like I was being mean or something, and that was when I really started to squirm. Why, if my sisters can get me to feeling mean or guilty, then it's all over. I'm too soft-hearted. I'll do anything to get rid of that feeling. And unfortunately, that night was no exception.

"Ah . . . I guess you can," I said, hoping that she would fall into a gopher hole before she could ask it.

"Hyrum, have you ever kissed a girl?"

"Whaaaaaaaaaaaaaat?"

"I said, Hyrum," and now she looked at me again, setting me to squirming even more, "have you ever kissed a girl?"

"Why, no . . . I, ah—"

And before I had time to stutter out another word, she leaned up and kissed me on the cheek. Not a big kiss, mind you. Just a very solid one.

Well, my mouth came open in shock, but nothing in the way of a scream for help would come out. Good grief! What was going on? This walking a girl home was getting clear out of hand. I pushed my hands deeper into my pockets and quickened my pace, but that didn't do very much good at all. We hadn't made it another fifty feet when she attacked again. Only this time it was a full frontal assault.

She tightened her grip on my sleeve, spun around in front of me, and threw her arms around my neck. Then with all the concentration she could muster she planted a kiss—and I don't mean just a little "Aunt Polly peck" either, but the whole full-grown outfit—right smack dab on my mouth. And I'll tell you, then I *knew* I'd never been kissed before!

For about twenty years or so I couldn't move or breathe or anything else, but then she released me and pulled away slightly and looked up at me with those big eyes of hers shining in the moonlight, and to tell you the truth, I just couldn't handle it any longer.

It's pretty embarrassing to admit this, but like Joseph in Potiphar's house I gave one long wild yelp that expressed everything I had ever felt before, shoved her arms aside, and then I got me out of there. I did feel bad to see her lose her balance and tumble toward the ditch at my sudden departure, but my sorrow was dulled to a remarkable degree by my sense of relief. I hoped that she didn't fall into the ditch, for it was about three feet deep, and full, but then she was a big girl. She could get out by herself. As for me, I didn't even touch the ground until I got to our barn on the other side of town.

As I hunted up the stool and got out the milk pail, I was actually glad that I still had the chores to do. I just couldn't bring myself to walk into that house yet, not with my head still spinning as it was.

Slowly my breathing and heartbeat climbed down out of the loft and I started to milk, all the time rehearsing in my mind everything that had happened. I was just coming to the part where her eyes were shining at me in the moonlight when I heard a noise. Well, my heart dropped clear out through the bottom of my feet, it shook me up so badly. But when I dared to look, I found it was just the cat, who was acting about as scared as I was. So I squirted some warm milk in her face, and then we both settled down.

Except for that kiss, I reflected, the whole evening had been great. I mean, I was still socially retarded, but with a little practice I might have a chance.

"You know, old gal," I said to Hepsi, "it's hard to figure out girls. They simply make no sense, no sense at all! But I'm sure glad Pa bought that horse. I surely am. If it wasn't for that horse, I might never have been kissed, scary as it was!"

4

The Raid

"All right, boys," Deputy McNeely said softly, "move up quiet now. You know how important this is to Marshal Clawson. Hank, you and George get around behind and watch the back. Bill, you take Parsons and watch the sides. We don't want this bird to slip away from his roost unseen."

"McNeely, are you sure he's in there?"

"Yeah, I'm sure. Clawson told me he was; that Sorenson kid saw him go in late last night, and you know we've seen no movement at all this morning. Soderberg's in there, all right. We just have to smoke him out."

"Hey, there's a light!"

"Sure enough. That Mormonite is up early, isn't he? No matter, though. Okay, boys, get in position. I'll fire a shot at 5:00 A.M. sharp, and when you hear it, break in that back door quick. We'll be coming through the front door at the same time, and between us we'll have that blasted Mormonite polyg dead to rights."

In the predawn darkness, McNeely and the other deputies quietly closed in on the home of Bishop Soderberg. In all there were five of them, each heavily armed and expecting trouble—and that may have been why, when there was none, they did what they did.

At five o'clock sharp the sound of a gunshot echoed through the sleeping streets of Aspen Wells. An instant later, Polly Soderberg, who was getting ready to feed her three-month-old daughter Sarah, saw the front door of her home smashed open and her parlor fill quickly with armed men.

Hastily the house was searched, but Soderberg was not there. Nor had be been since midnight, when he had slipped past the eyes of spying neighbors to spend the night with his second wife, Victoria.

Instead they found Polly's daughter Elinor, sixteen, and her son Ernest, who was even younger. Roughly the two were pulled from their beds and pushed downstairs into the parlor, where their mother was being held at gunpoint.

"All right," Deputy McNeely shouted, "where's he at? We know he's in here, and we've got a warrant for his arrest. Now where is he?"

All three remained silent, and it was then that the men, frustrated, went contrary to standing orders and became physically abusive.

When a frantic Ernest, an eye swollen almost closed, found his father almost two hours later, the story he told was almost beyond belief.

Sick at heart, hurting, and more angry than he had ever been in his life, Bishop Soderberg ran desperately through the fields and up to the smashed-in back door of his home. As he burst into the parlor, the sight that met his eyes was overwhelming. Furniture, some of it broken beyond repair, was scattered everywhere. Window panes were broken out, lamps were shattered, the smell of coal oil was everywhere, and in the midst of the rubble he found his wife and his daughter Elinor resolutely cleaning up the room, their faces tear-streaked and grim. Then they explained to the angry bishop, between sobs, what the deputies had done and why.

Jons Soderberg did what he could to help and comfort, and it wasn't long before both Victoria and Hattie, his other wives, were there also, sharing the grief, the anger, and the despair.

Later in the day he saddled his Belgian stud and rode slowly up past his mill and to the Big Springs. The springs were nestled in a little cove at the base of the mountain, and in the entire valley he knew of nowhere that was so quiet, so cool, and so serene. The Big Springs was where he came with all his weighty problems, for he had found that the very atmosphere helped him feel more close to God. The quietness calmed his soul, and the stillness helped him to place things in proper perspective.

For some time he sat on his horse in silence, watching the crystal water gushing out of the rocks. The spring was immense, and had been, according to the older residents, the subject of an interesting prophecy by President Brigham Young. Apparently the first year Brigham had sent settlers to the area the spring had about dried up, and that forced all but two or three to leave for other locations. When Brother Brigham heard of it, passing through that fall, he had stood in his wagon and told the people that as long as they lived their religion there would always be ample water in that spring to meet the needs of the community. Interestingly, Aspen Wells had grown over the years, and so had the spring. Each year, even when there had been drought in the valley, that spring had put forth enough water for the community. Between seven and eight hundred people used the spring now for their entire water supply, and there was plenty for them.

In the west, water was life. One lived where one could get water, or one didn't live. Brigham Young had told the people that no one owned the water, that it was the Lord's, and all who needed it should have access to it. Not everyone believed him, though, or felt as he did. One such man came to Aspen Wells and determined that the Big Springs would be a likely source of wealth. In Pine Canyon, just north of the springs, he dug a tunnel, intending to intercept the water and then sell it.

Stories conflicted about exactly what happened, but the way the bishop heard it the fellow dug in quite a way. The citizens complained to Brother Brigham, and he warned the man away, predicting dire consequences. The man ignored the counsel, and shortly afterward met with an accident in which he lost his arm at the sawmill up Ephraim Canyon. Of course that stopped the digging.

And so the stories went. Whether they were all true or not Jons Soderberg did not know. Nor did he feel that it was important. The important thing was that the people believed them, and shaped their lives accordingly. Brigham Young and the others who had led the Church were prophets; he himself knew that to be true. But a prophet, to be most effective in carrying out the Lord's work, must have a believing people behind him, people who would be willing to do as he felt impressed they should, even when it was difficult or was contrary to their personal wishes. If a man was a prophet indeed, then it could not be that he would be inspired only about religion. One who had actual access to the mind and will of the Lord should be inspired regarding all aspects of the lives of the Lord's children, whether they were political, social, economic, or spiritual. And so the prophets of the latter days had spoken, though there were many who felt inclined to disregard their counsel. The stories helped, though, for they taught lessons secondhand that, learned firsthand by all the people, would have become far too expensive and time-consuming. The bishop wondered whether the story about the Pine Canyon tunnel was all true, and, if so, whether the man's accident was indeed divinely engineered. He grinned a little as he thought how ludicrous it would be for the Lord to cut off the arms of all the men and women who had ever become a little greedy. One sufficed; word spread, and many learned the lesson.

But what about his problem? What about polygamy and persecution? He had done what he had been told to do, both in the taking of plural wives and in the avoiding of the federal marshals. The prophet had promised him that if he lived his religion it would all work out. Well, he had tried, had been doing his best, he felt, but now the law had taken it to him. What was a man to do?

"Father," he said softly, "thou gavest me a family, and thou gavest me the responsibility of caring for them and protecting them. Thou also called me as bishop, and gave me the responsibility of conducting my life in a manner that would be above reproach. But, Father, today my heart is as black as midnight, and for the first time in my life I want to do murder! They've hurt my wife and daughter and son, and as their husband and father I want to strike back! Oh, how I want to strike back!

"Tell me, Heavenly Father. How is it that thou wouldst ever want a man like me for thy bishop? The scripture says thou knowest the end from the beginning, so I know thou knewest this was going to happen, and how I was going to feel. Dear God, please help me. Help me to clear my heart, help me to think clearly, help me to be the kind of man I told thee I would be. Help me. . . ."

For the remainder of that afternoon the bishop sought the help of the Lord, and later that night, when he returned home to Polly and Elinor, he spoke reverently of a marvelous spiritual experience. There, in the midst of his anxiety and his frustration, he had felt a spirit of calmness settle upon him like a blanket, filling his whole soul with peace and an understanding that justice would ultimately be done.

In the days that followed, the incident with the marshals was never mentioned outside of the home. Two weeks later, when Baby Sarah died, the neighbors thought it was because of some disease, though no explanation was given. No one outside the family ever knew that the bishop and his wives and children blamed Sarah's death on the shock her mother received at the hands of the marshals. The emotional upheaval brought on by that incident, they felt, caused Polly's milk to dry up, and her little daughter slowly starved to death.

Bitterness toward the law, its founders, and its upholders naturally grew, and Jons Soderberg and his families vowed with a fierce determination that they would never, willingly or otherwise, submit themselves to the power and authority of the mob that called itself the law.

5

Soap Day

A few days after the raid on our Big House, where Aunt Polly lived, Ma shook me awake earlier than usual.

"Hyrum," she whispered, "get dressed quickly, and hurry downstairs as soon as you've said your prayers."

"Why, Ma? What's going on?"

"Soap day, Hyrum. Did you forget?"

"Oh, no!" I groaned. "Not soap day again! Ma, can't the girls do it?"

"Hyrum, I'm ashamed of you! You know those little girls can't stir that thick soap or move that heavy kettle around. Now, hurry so we can do it in the cool of the morning. I don't want to spend all day on it."

Well, I dragged myself out of bed, threw a few words towards heaven, though with my attitude I doubt that they got past the ceiling, pulled on my clothes, and stumbled out to do the chores. I got the pigs, chickens, and ducks fed and watered, and then I went to war with Hepsi.

That morning Hepsi had a sore teat, but in my frame of mind I couldn't have cared less. I just tucked her tail underneath my left knee and commenced squeezing and pulling. At the first good pull on the sore teat, however, Hepsi jerked her tail out and popped me on the side of the head with it. Now, normally that wouldn't be so bad, but it just happened that her tail was filled with cockleburs and dried mud and dung from our recent rain, so you can guess how that felt. Angrily I jerked her tail back under my knee, took more ungentle pulls at her udder, and that blasted cow popped me with her tail again.

"Doggone it, Hepsi!" I shouted, giving her a look that would make an icicle feel feverish. "Cut it out! If you hit me with your tail one more time, I promise you a whole lot of grief!"

For a while I milked while Hepsi and I stared each other in the eye. I knew then that she understood exactly what I was saying, and I know it now. She knew exactly who was boss, and she wouldn't—

Whap!

That third slap was by far the hardest, and I was so mad that I just hauled back and slugged her in the side, as hard as I could hit.

"There! Take that, you ornery no-account good-for-nothing miserable excuse for a flea-infested bovine hay-burner! You dirty sway-backed despicable udder-slung—*Owwww!*"

And that miserable cow retaliated by planting her monstrous splayed hoof right on top of my left foot, smashing it forty feet into the ground.

"Hepsi!" I screeched, jerking and pulling on my foot, trying to get it out from under several tons of ugly beef. "*Hepsi!* You low-down, mean.... *Get off my foot!*"

With all my weight I pushed against her leg, and finally she shifted, allowing me to pull my mangled foot loose. Really upset now, I grabbed that sore teat and pulled with all my might, determined to show her that no cow-critter could come it over a human the way she was trying to do.

Well, she kicked at me then, but I anticipated that move and leaned back, laughing at her feeble efforts. Trouble was, I forgot for a moment that I was dealing with Hepsi, and I had an absolute knowledge that she was the smartest doggone cow in the whole county.

Quick as a wink, before I could do or say anything, that blasted cow did the worst thing that she could possibly have done.

I had forgotten the milk bucket, which was nearly full and still sitting directly under her. With malice gleaming in her eyes she turned and looked at me and then lifted her foot high into the air. Desperately I lunged, knowing what she was about to do. But I was too late, forever too late, and in an agony of defeated spirit I watched as she plunked her filthy hoof down in the exact center of that pail of milk. For about a hundred years she let the warm milk soak the straw and you-know-what-else off of her hoof, turning our milk a kind of greenish brown. Then gently she withdrew it, being careful not to overturn the pail.

The war ended right there, with our cow the victor, and me, as usual, defeated and in trouble. You see, I knew that Hepsi understood how badly Ma needed that milk, and she knew full well that when I came home without it I would be in real trouble. That was why, when she was angry with me, she would step in the milk. She never did it with Pa, or with Ma, or with any of the others. Just me. And she never did it when the bucket was empty, either. She only did it when it was full. That cow was so mean and so smart that it was scary.

Well, I cleaned out the bucket, stripped Hepsi, gave what there was of the milk to Ma, took my verbal licking, bolted down my mush, and went out to get started with the soap.

Several days earlier I'd had the job of making potash lye from our ashes, so I should have been expecting that soap day would come along. Ma said, in regard to the lye, that she preferred apple wood ash because lye from apple wood made the whitest soap. But Pa told her he wasn't about to cut down our orchard so she could have white soap. So we used scrub oak out of the hills, which wasn't as white but which made the strongest lye a body ever saw.

We extracted it by filling a tub with ashes and then pouring boiling water into it. As the ashes settled we added more ashes and more boiling water, and then we let it steep for a day or two. Finally I'd draw off some of the water, and if it would float a fresh egg we knew it had enough lye. Then we'd boil it down until the water was gone, leaving what Ma called Black Salts. This we also cooked, heating it until the black was burned out and we had a whitish powder which was potash lye.

Compared to making soap, making lye was easy. I mean, have you ever spent a day, when the sun was hot enough to wither a fence-post, stirring boiling grease over a hot fire with lye fumes burning your nose? If you have, then you know why I groaned when Ma told me it was soap day. There was nothing that I hated worse than making soap on a hot summer day.

I got the fire going out behind our log home, got out the big kettle, and finally had it situated so the fire was around it rather than under it. Ma said that prevented the soap from burning.

"Now what, Ma?" I shouted, always feeling uneasy about the recipe for making soap. In a moment she was there, and we set about making hard lye soap.

"First, Hyrum, bring seven and a half gallons of water to a boil. When it's boiling, dissolve three pounds of potash lye in the water, and then call me. I'll be inside getting up a program for sisters' meeting Thursday night."

"Thursday," I thought as I fed the fire. "Fast day again. It hasn't been too long since I dreaded that day like a plague, but now I don't feel that way. Hyrum, old boy, like your Ma says, maybe you are growing up."

I thought about it then, remembering the feelings of agony and hunger I endured working all day Thursday and then sitting through an eternally long meeting that night. Two months before, though, I was sitting in fast meeting thinking about nothing in particular when I had the strangest feeling that I ought to stand up and say something. Naturally I rebelled, preferring to be thought of as a fool rather than to stand up and remove all doubts. But the feeling wouldn't let me alone, and after a little while I stood up and said some things about how I felt about my folks and about the Church. Right then I got choked up and started watering the pew in front of me, and I surely did feel foolish. But I also felt something else, something that I don't know how to explain. It was the hottest and most special feeling I've ever had, and I felt like I was going to explode, it was so big. And right then I knew, I mean I really *knew*, that Joseph Smith was a prophet and that the church he helped restore was the true Church.

I used to wake up nights and wonder what I'd do if I died and got over there and the apostle Peter or someone told me our church wasn't true. For the last two months I hadn't wondered that. You see, the Holy Ghost gave me a testimony. That's how come I was crying and choking and all that. Pa told me that was how the Holy Ghost affected people, jumping up and down on their heartstrings, so to speak. He said it was surely nothing to be ashamed of; he'd irrigated a few pews and pulpits himself, time to time, and he felt proud that the Lord loved him enough to give him that witness. I did too, and now I looked forward to fasting and attending fast meeting, watching other folks feel the same feelings I'd felt. In fact, I was even starting to feel tolerant of old Sister Adolfson, who rattled on every month about her illnesses and her four hundred or so kids. You see, it dawned on me that with all her rattling on, she was just trying to put into words all those feelings that I'd had and had stumbled over myself. I was just able to get the job done quicker, is all. And for that I was thankful.

When the water finally boiled I added the lye, careful to be way back so it wouldn't spit or splash on me. When it had dissolved, Ma came out and slowly added nine pounds of mutton tallow which she had rendered earlier. Meanwhile I stirred and stirred and stirred, the fire burned and burned and burned, the sun got hotter and hotter, and I got more miserable by the minute.

To make myself feel better I tried thinking of happy things, like Ida Mae, for instance. But somehow I just couldn't think of her while I was stirring Ma's boiling lye soap. Now, witches I could think of, and hell and the devil and the Great Salt Lake desert and that sort of thing. But I surely couldn't keep my mind on Ida Mae. Why in tarnation did it take so long for the lye and fat to saponify?

"Hyrum!" Ma called, surprising me out of my gloom.

"What?"

"Drop some soap on the plate, and tell me what it does."

I did; it turned milky around the edges, so Ma had me add a little more lye. When that was finally cooked in, the droplets on the plate remained clear, so I added a pound and a half of salt, which separated the soap from the water and caused the soap to rise to the surface.

I was stirring on that when Ma came out and put her arm around my waist. It hadn't been too long since she'd put her arm around my shoulder, but now when we stood side by side I looked down upon her. Somehow that made her seem little, which was hard for me to get used to. It made me want to ... well, protect her, I guess. She just seemed so little and so helpless, though I knew that was silly. Why, she could outwork me any day of the week. One day I just watched her, and in that one day she milked the cows, killed and cleaned five chickens, made noodles, churned up some butter, pulled a carriage nearly full of beans, cooked up three meals, helped Pa set posts for a fence, and then got cleaned up and went with Pa to a dance down at the Pavilion. I've also seen her hitch up the team and plow and harrow our field, dig ditches, sew up all kinds of clothes, shear sheep, card and spin the wool, fast days at a time for someone in our ward who was sick, and chew out Brother Anderson for taking the water out of our ditch before our turn was up. (And did he repent quick? Well, I hope to shout he did! No one could face up to Ma when her wrath was up.) Funny thing was, she smiled while she was telling him off, and I really believe that Brother Anderson walked away from Ma feeling happy as well as repentant.

That was why I felt silly thinking that Ma was helpless. I knew better, everyone else knew better, and yet I still felt that way. I couldn't help it. Pa says it's natural for a man to feel protective of a woman, and he says the good Lord made women small and soft so men would want to be protective. Ma told me that the Lord fixed women up so they would want to care for a man and would need a man's protection, emotionally as well as physically. The Lord did it so that men and women would get together and stay that way. Men need to provide for and to protect, women need to care about and to be protected. It's as simple as that, for God made us that way. Pa says that men and women are equal in that way only: They need each other. Beyond that, this equal rights business, like Arizona is stewing about, is pretty much nonsense. Up until the Edmunds-Tucker Bill passed, Mormon women in Utah had the right to vote just like the men. Pa says that Arizona is trying to decide whether to give women the franchise, but Ma says it makes no never-mind with her. She says she doesn't want to be equal with men. It's all right to vote, but beyond that she doesn't want to stoop to the level men usually live on.

So anyway, Ma put her arm around my waist and squeezed, looked up at me with her eyes full of tears of gratitude, and suddenly that old soap job didn't seem so bad after all.

"Hyrum, thank you so much! I know this is a miserable job, but, son, it still must be done. I'm so thankful that Jons and I were blessed with such a fine man for a son. I hope you know how much your father and sisters and I love you.

"Now, Hyrum, old Sister Nielson died this morning, and Polly, Victoria, and I are going down to hold a wake for her. We'll keep her body packed in ice today, and then other sisters will take over until the funeral. Can you set the soap out, cut it, and get it drying alone?"

"Sure, Ma."

"Thank you, son. I surely love you."

"Yeah, Ma. I love you, too."

A little later Aunt Victoria and Aunt Polly drove up in their cart, Ma climbed aboard, and all three of Pa's wives rode off together, smiling and talking and hugging each other just like they were real sisters. I was thinking on that, wondering at the marvel of those three women loving each other like they did when they shared the same husband, when I heard hoofbeats coming down the lane. I stood up to look, and it was Pa and Ernest riding Pa's new horse.

"Hi, Pa," I called. "Ma just left with Aunt Polly and Aunt Victoria. Didn't you see them? Sister Nielson passed away and they were going there."

"I saw them, Hyrum. And I heard about Sister Nielson. It's sad, but she surely has been ill. Hattie says you've been stirring soap since early this morning. Is that right?"

"Yeah, I reckon. Though it feels longer than that."

"I'll bet it does. How much longer before you finish? I'd like you to come up to the mill with me."

"Well, Ma wants the soap all set out and cut up into squares. That will take a little while."

"Ernest, can you cut soap?" Pa asked.

Ernest nodded vigorously, so Pa set him to cutting up my soap, freeing me so I could go up to the mill. I was also minding my little sisters, so Ernest was assigned that task, too, and in a moment I was up behind Pa on that big Belgian stud.

We rode for a time in silence, and to tell the truth I was surprised how smooth that big horse moved. I really enjoyed riding him, and believe me, that was saying something. I *never* enjoyed riding plugs!

As we passed the widow Nielson's place I saw Pa's horse and cart hitched out front, and that put me in mind of Ma, and Pa's other wives. Time to time, the past day or so, I'd been thinking about that, wondering about marriage and polygamy and having a wife or so, wondering what it was like. But that is a hard thing to ask someone about, so I hadn't done it. Now, though, with thoughts of Ida Mae pestering me constantly, I suddenly decided to ask Pa what being married and being a polygamist was like.

After I'd asked, Pa was quiet so long that I decided he hadn't heard me. I was about to ask him again when he finally spoke.

"Say," he asked, "what kind of a question is that from a fellow who three months ago didn't even like the thoughts of a girl?"

Well, I got red right away, and mumbled something about just wondering.

"Wouldn't have anything to do with Ida Mae Sorenson, would it?" Pa asked.

I was getting real fidgety by then, and was wishing with all my heart that I hadn't said anything. But then Pa jabbed me in the ribs with his elbow, squeezed my knee to death with his big hand, and answered me.

"Hy," he said, "being married is like different things on different days. Some days there isn't anything greater. Other days, well, a man wonders. He surely does. Still," and now Pa grinned back at me, "I'd say that most of the time there is nothing better than being married to a good woman. And, of course, being married to three of them is just three times better. Right?

"But, Hy, how does a man tell his son what it's like? I don't know. Most of the time it's a happy, calm, relaxed, comfortable feeling. My wives help me to feel comfortable and relaxed, for with them I don't have to be anyone other than who I am. They know me for that, and they have me convinced that they love me in spite of what they know about me. With them I never have to pretend or impress, and that's a very comfortable feeling.

"It's not an easy thing for a man and a woman to learn to live together, because men and women are so different in so many ways. And the obvious physical difference is just part of that, Hy. There are basic differences in terms of feelings and emotions, too. All these things must be dealt with when a man and a woman are married. Of course, they must be dealt with prior to that also, when boys and girls begin courting. Right?''

"Yeah, I reckon. But Pa, I never knew they were different. I mean—well—''

"That's all right, Hy. I think I know what you're saying.''

"Well, how are girls different, then?''

"That is a good question. I hope I can answer it. For one thing, women are closer to their feelings than most men seem to be. They tend to cry more readily, they get their feelings hurt more easily, and so on. And, they like to talk more about their feelings than men do. As a bishop and a husband, I've encountered that situation right frequently.''

"Does that mean that women feel more things than men do?''

"Oh no, Hy! I don't think so. It's just that a woman's feelings seem closer to the surface than most men allow theirs to get. As men, we have to recognize that and deal with it when we associate with women.''

"How?''

"Boy, you are full of questions, aren't you? All right, here's one way. You and Jim and Lyman shove each other around a lot, in fun, showing that you care for each other. Right?''

"Yeah, I guess so.''

"Well, I wouldn't recommend that you do that sort of thing too often with young ladies, Hy. Ida Mae surely wouldn't think you liked her if you started slugging her and pushing her around.''

"Gee, Pa. I wouldn't do that with her."

"No, of course you wouldn't, because you understand some of the differences between men and women already."

"Are there any others?"

"Well, yes. But offhand I can't recall—wait a minute! There is one other difference you ought to understand."

"What?"

"It has to do with feelings again, Hy, but in a slightly different way. I've noticed you eyeballing the young gals lately. Why?"

"Huh?"

"Why do you look at the girls, Hy?"

"Oh, scrud, Pa. I don't know."

"Yes you do. Now why?"

"Well, because they're cute, I guess."

"Sure they are. But I've also noticed one or two of the girls looking at you. Why do you think they do that?"

"I don't know, but it sure ain't because I'm cute."

"Yes, that would be stretching the imagination some, wouldn't it?"

Pa grinned at me then, so I knew he was funning. Sort of. Thing was, he was right in a way, and for the first time I got to cogitating about it.

"Hy," Pa continued, "men are generally stimulated by what they see. That's why girls look cute to men, and why men look at them. It's exciting.

"Girls, however, aren't usually stimulated or excited by what they see so much as they are by what they feel. If a woman feels warmth, or love, or security from a man, she is attracted to him. And it doesn't seem to matter much what he looks like. He is still exciting to her."

"Golly, Pa, I never knew that."

"No, I didn't expect you did. But the Brethren in Salt Lake City know it. That's why they've asked girls to be modest in their dress and in their actions. If a girl is immodest or inappropriate, she makes it awfully tough for a fellow to keep his thoughts pure.

"And, of course, that is also why the Brethren have counseled us men to be modest and restrained in our physical relationships with women other than our wives."

"I don't understand, Pa."

"Hy, let me explain it this way. When most boys kiss and hug and so on, especially when they are quite young, they are usually only satisfying selfish desires. It's not likely that they are thinking much about the girl, or about building lasting relationships with her.

"With young ladies, thoughts and feelings are entirely different. Hyrum, from my experience as a bishop I've learned that when most girls become physically involved, it isn't because they are thrilled and excited about the prospects of touching a boy. It's because they desire the security that seems to come with touching. They want a lasting relationship, for that means security. Many girls believe, usually mistakenly, that excessive physical closeness will result in such a commitment that will lead to security.

"As an example, a boy often will hold a girl's hand for the sheer excitement of holding hands. The girl thinks this means that the boy likes her. Actually, all it means is that he likes to hold her hand. If I could somehow teach this to the girls in our ward, I'm certain there would be fewer moral problems.

"Anyway, Hy, when boys insist on being physical, that can cause girls to have as much trouble with the purity of their thoughts as boys have when girls are immodest. And that is why both boys and girls are to a certain extent responsible for helping each other to control their thoughts and emotions. It seems to always come back to the Savior's Golden Rule, which tells us that we ought to really care about each other. Does that make sense?"

"Yeah, though I hadn't thought of it before."

"Well, I seem to have gone off on a tangent. Your question was about what it was like to be married, wasn't it? And I can best answer that by saying that it is like any other job. If a man buckles down to it and works at it with all his heart, developing true love, it will be one of the most satisfying and rewarding things he can ever do. If he doesn't, then it's likely that he'll be miserable."

"But, Pa, how can you love three women? And how can they love you and each other? I mean, I like Ida Mae, but if I saw her with another fellow I'd be upset. How come Ma and Aunt Polly and Aunt Victoria don't get jealous?"

Pa chuckled and didn't answer right off, but when he did, his answer surprised me.

"They do, Hy. They do. Jealousy is a human trait, and all three of my wives are surely human. I recollect the night that Elder Daniel H. Wells asked Polly and me to enter into plural marriage. That was a tough decision for both of us, but Polly is a very righteous woman with a strong desire to be obedient. Ultimately, believe it or not, *she* convinced *me* that we should do it. Together we decided that Victoria would be a likely second wife, we invited her to Sunday dinner, and I began courting her. Hyrum, I'll never forget the look on Polly's face when we left the Endowment House in Salt Lake City the day Victoria and I were sealed. Victoria and I climbed into the buggy to begin our honeymoon, Polly stood on the boardwalk watching us, and, Hyrum, riding away from her was one of the hardest things I've ever had to do. Talk about a woman conquering jealousy, striving for a righteous attitude!

"From time to time since then there have been difficulties, of course, but all four of us do our best to make those difficulties minimal. For instance, I'll never leave Polly's home to stay with your mother if Polly and I are having problems. If I were to do that, jealousies could really develop. Neither will one of my wives pressure me to do something if I have a prior commitment with another of them. We all agreed on this, and it works out very well.

"With three wives, a man surely learns fairness. If I were to ever start showing favoritism for one or another of them, the other two would see to it that I became the most miserable man alive. And believe me, Hyrum, women have the ability to make men miserable if they so desire. So I do my best to be fair. I buy cloth by the bolt and divide it into three equal lengths, and I try to spend equal time in each home. Another thing is that each of my wives is given a quarter once a week so that she can go down to the barbershop and take a bath. Now you'll have to admit that is being very fair and lenient. Most husbands don't do that.''

I grinned, thinking of the last bath I had there. It was a hot steamy room in the rear of the barbershop with no windows, so at least it was private. The other thing is that it was the only bathtub in town. Still, I preferred the hole in the creek up by the Swedish Temple. The air was better there.

"So, Hyrum," Pa continued, "I do love each of them. Each of them I love in a different way, yet I sincerely feel that I love all three of them equally.

"Anyway, how can I explain what it's like being married to three women? I don't even know if I understand myself what it's like. They're so different from each other. Polly is quiet, but is an expert organizer. Victoria is much more vocal and is very skilled with her hands. But when I'm with her I always feel like I am in a whirlpool, kind of dizzy with things spinning all around me. Victoria is not an organized person.

"Then there is Hattie. Hyrum, your mother is the softest, most kind and gentle woman I've ever known. She has more love in her little finger than I'll ever have. That's why I called her to be president of the Relief Society. Polly would run a tighter ship, Victoria would do a much better job conducting meetings, but Hattie simply loves and cares her way into the hearts of the sisters here in Aspen Wells. Still, don't let your mother's softness fool you. She's tougher than nails, and she's rolling thunder when she's upset. Do you remember last spring when I took all three of my wives out to Jericho with me to shear sheep?''

"Yes."

"Well, in fun I challenged them to see which one could shear the most sheep, and I promised that whichever one of them did, she would be the one who sat beside me on our way home. The others would have to ride in back with the wool. Well, they laughed about it and things started out pretty normal. Polly went right to work; Victoria couldn't catch a sheep, and then when she finally did she couldn't find her shears; and Hattie wouldn't catch one because she felt sorry for them and thought we were hurting them. But then one of

52

the others said something to Hattie about her thinking she was too good and too dainty to shear, and you never saw a woman get so busy so quickly. She didn't say a word. She just smiled at all of us and fairly flew over those sheep. And when it was all over, your mother rode home beside me.

"Of course, you know how we do things as a family—picnicking, fishing, and so on. And I try and involve all of you as much as possible in my businesses. That's why I'm taking you to our mill with me. I want to teach you how to run the new roller process I just had installed. Doing things together builds family closeness, and, Hyrum, having a strong and closely united family is what life is all about."

"But, Pa, don't you ever feel . . . well, funny? I mean, isn't it embarrassing to have three wives and a whole passel of kids tagging behind you?"

"Feel funny? Well, sometimes I do. I felt a little foolish the day Elder Snow sustained me as bishop. He asked for my wife and me to come up to the stand, and everyone laughed when all three of my wives stood at once and then couldn't decide how to line up in the aisle."

"Golly, Pa, wasn't that embarrassing?"

"Well, I should smile it was, especially when all those folks started laughing. I think I was red clear down to my toenails."

"What did you do?"

"What could I do? Elder Snow had asked us to come up, so we had no choice but to go. So I lined those women up single file, the shortest one first, and I followed them up to the stand. And, Hyrum, it seems like I have been following them ever since."

Pa grinned then, and I did, too, knowing how Ma would bend over backward to do what Pa asked her to do. I also knew that Pa would do almost anything Ma asked him to do. Seemed to me like nobody in our family followed anybody, unless of course you counted the Lord. Pretty much I think we all followed each other.

"Pa, do you think I'll ever be a polygamist?"

"Well, son, I don't know. I don't know how much longer our Church will be able to practice it, with all the pressures we're getting from Washington. Our leaders are underground, our property has been confiscated, all of us have been disfranchised, and none of us dare hardly even live. Of course, this is the Lord's Church, and he is powerful enough to overturn all the governments on the earth if he is of a mind to do it. And that would certainly solve the problem. Thing is, it has been my experience that God most generally leaves problem solving to us mortals. If he does that with polygamy, I couldn't guess what will happen.

"One thing I do know, though. I will follow the Brethren, and do whatever they tell me to. If we retain polygamy, I will support it to the death. If we are told to cease the practice of it, then I will take no more wives. Beyond that, after seeing how the law has treated me and my family, I will never submit to them. I will die first! Now, as for you, my boy, I'd recommend a few years and one wife before you start worrying about a whole passel of them. Wouldn't you agree?''

"Yeah,'' I said, "I agree.'' And wouldn't it be nice, I thought, if I could someday marry Ida Mae? Golly, she is something!

For the rest of the way up to the mill Pa talked about the crops in the fields we were passing. But I only half listened, for I was day-dreaming about Ida Mae, wondering if she would support me if the Lord ever called me to be a polygamist. I wondered if she could be as strong as Aunt Polly had been.

At last we turned into the lane leading up to the mill, and Pa turned back for a final look at Aspen Wells. As he did so I glimpsed, behind some bushes ahead of us, the piebald gelding of Deputy Clawson.

"Pa!'' I yelped, flinging myself off of the horse. "It's the Feds, over by the mill!''

Pa turned, took one quick look, wheeled Ingersol around and was gone in a cloud of dust. In that same instant Deputy Clawson came boiling out of the hawbushes after Pa.

"Get out of the way, kid! Blast it, get out of the way! Soderberg, you low-life coward, hold up there! You're under arrest!''

Well, you know about my bad leg. I tried to get out of his way, I really did. Thing was, I somehow hobbled right into the path of that cross-eyed gelding, and when I got there my leg gave out and I lost my balance. Naturally, I had to wave my arms around a bit to keep from falling, and I reckon I got a mite carried away hollering for help to get away from that stampeding horse.

Of course all that racket and jumping around must have somehow spooked the gelding, for it took off through the hawbushes like it was loco, pitching and bucking and giving the marshal a ride he'll not likely forget. The marshal wasn't silent, either, but I'd best not repeat what it was he was saying. Suffice it to say that I laughed until my sides hurt, and then I walked home, taking a shortcut, sort of, down to the other end of town past Ida Mae's home. The next day when I saw Pa we had a good laugh together. And that was pretty much how it was being the son of a Mormon polygamist.

6

Birds of the Roost

In 1888, Green River, Utah, was known for two things: its frigid winter winds and its proximity to the infamous area known as Robbers' Roost. Several miles southwest of Green River City, the land climbed gradually to the top of the San Rafael Swell, a waterless black horseshoe of a rock nearly eight thousand feet high and about eighty miles long. This was the Roost country.

The south side of the swell dropped steeply into the bitter and alkaline waters of the Muddy and Dirty Devil rivers, while the north side of the swell dropped into the San Rafael River. This in turn wound a snakelike course through the tortured San Rafael country, a land which old-timers claimed was used by the Lord as the blueprint for hell, until at last it spilled itself into the murky waters of the Green River.

Across the Green from its confluence with the San Rafael was a sandy bottom nearly a quarter of a mile wide and maybe three times that in length. It was surrounded on all sides by high sandstone cliffs, was filled with huge old cottonwoods, squawbrush, and greasewood, and the Green at that point had a bottom that was quicksand. In short, it was a lonely and inaccessible area.

Under the cottonwoods, back from the river and beneath an overhanging sandstone ledge, stood an ancient and decrepit cabin. It was windowless, except for the chinks between the rough-hewn logs, and its only door hung crookedly from one hinge, cabin and door resembling nothing so much in character as the three men who sat within.

Their names, which do not matter that much, were Jack Moore, Jim Wall, and John Griffith. Locally, however, they were known as the Boss, Silvertip, and Blue John. Moore, a tall young man with black curly hair, commanding presence, and an overpowering urge for dishonesty, was the Boss simply because he was. Wall, the oldest of the three, was called Silvertip because of the graying around his temples and because of his heavy shoulders and rolling walk, which was much like that of a grizzly bear. Griffith, less a cowboy than the others, was known as Blue John because he had one blue eye while the other was brown. Blue John was an excellent cook and a master with teams and wagons, while Silvertip, not long on intelligence, was still an excellent horse thief. Together, the three of them were anything but a trio of square dealers. And at the moment, Jack Moore, the fiery-tempered boss, was obviously upset with the other two.

"All right, Silvertip," he was saying, unmistakable anger and disgust in his voice, "lead that past me one more time. I sent you to the mines at Cisco to get this horse I heard about. You did get it, but on the way back you sold it. Have I got it right?"

"Yeah, Boss, you got it right as rain. Plucking that nag out of the corral in Cisco was a job I could do surer than a belch after supper. 'Twern't nothing to it. Then Blue John lifts this wagon, we tie our horses to the back, hitch that plug to the wagon, and leave town with nobody the wiser."

"Why didn't you ride the stallion out?"

"Boss, that ain't no riding horse. It's a plug, and nobody rides work plugs. You'd oughta know that."

Moore got a pained look on his face, rolled his eyes heavenward, and said, "When they was pourin' in brains, someone joggled their arm.'' He went on, ''All right Blue John, you hitched the stallion to the wagon and got out of town first-rate. Now you take it from there.''

''Sure, Boss. Like Silvertip said, it all went too easy. And you know I ain't no riding cowboy. That's why we hitched up to the wagon. Why, with a wagon under me I can make a hoss stand up and dance. And that's what the stallion did all day long. He just danced.

''That night we was camped on the Sevier when someone hollered out of the darkness that the posse from Cisco was hot on the trail of the hombres who took their blooded Belgian stallion. That was the first we knowed it was blooded. So we doused our fire and heard the posse go past in the night.

''Next day I pulled the shoes off the horse and we headed north, up through Sanpete, hoping to shake the posse. But somehow they heard about us and was dusting along at a pretty good clip just a few miles back. That was when we ditched the wagon, and that there gave us a little breather, but we knowed it wouldn't be for long. Them fellers surely did want that horse back. So we was hightailing it up past Ephraim awondering what to do when here comes this Mormon bishop all set on buying our horse.

'' 'Well,' I says to Silvertip, 'this here looks an awful lot like the hand of providence. That there posse is making it hotter'n a burnt boot for us, but I reckon someone up there don't want nobody shortening our stake ropes. I also reckon he wants this here Mormon to enjoy all the blessings a hoss like this one can bring him, posse and all. And Silvertip,' I said, 'if heaven is so set on this man having this here blooded plug, then we ought to set a heavenly price on him.'

''Silvertip, he allowed as how we was using plumb good sense in shaking our tails at that hoss and skedaddling on out of there. So I says, 'Mr. Bishop, sir, this here animal is a highly prized blooded Belgian stallion. He belongs to our boss, but I'd be a mite shy of the truth if I wasn't to say that there is a whole passel of fellers who right this minute wish they were here getting this horse instead of you.'

''Well, the bishop, he comments on the fine points of the hoss, and then he looks in his mouth and asks us for a price. So I look at Silvertip, wink, and say, 'Mr. Bishop, sir, when a man looks over a hoss the way you've just done, then I know that there same gent is as wise as a tree full of owls, and there ain't no use in trying to pull the wool over his eyes. No, sir, Mr. Bishop, sir. You know the value of that blooded stud as well as I do myself, and there wouldn't be no point in quibbling over the price, not for either of us. We understand each other, we do, and that's why I'm willing to sell this beautiful animal to you for the fair price of two thousand dollars gold.'

" 'Sixteen hundred,' says the bishop, and afore you know it we had shook on eighteen hundred dollars gold. It took him about an hour to round up the money, and that is what is setting on the table here before you.' '

For a long moment there was silence in the cabin as Moore sat and eyed the two before him. A fly buzzed in the shade of the room, and Blue John stirred restlessly, uncertain of what his boss was thinking.

Suddenly Moore grinned and spoke. "Eighteen hundred dollars gold, huh? That is a lot of gold, to my way of thinking."

"You bet your pearl-handled pistols it is, Boss. Slickest hoss-trading we ever did."

"Eighteen hundred dollars gold. Say, Silvertip, which is highest, eighteen or twenty-six?"

"Uh, twenty-six is more, I think. Ain't it, Blue John?"

Blue John nodded, getting more nervous by the minute. He didn't know where the Boss was headed, but he had the feeling that he had the bit in his mouth and was being led.

"Silvertip," Moore continued, "I swear you are as chuckle-headed as a prairie pup with the mumps. And you, Blue John, you can't even use stupidity as an excuse. I sent you boys for that horse, that particular horse, for a reason. And that reason was that I know a rancher over near Telluride what will give me twenty-six hundred dollars gold for that blooded Belgian. What I am saying, boys, is that you just cost me eight hundred dollars gold. Do you savvy?"

The grin was gone now, and both men knew they were in big trouble. They'd been around the Boss long enough to know that he didn't carry his pearl-handled pistols for decoration. Moore was tough as boot leather and mean as a barrel full of rattlers, and one time they'd seen him go ten days with a dislocated shoulder without complaint, get it set, and then rob the sawbones who set it.

"Gee, Boss, we didn't know. Honest we didn't. I—"

Moore reached across the table, grabbed Silvertip's shirt, and yanked him forward, at the same time drawing his pistol to cover Blue John, who quietly lifted his hands and backed up against the wall.

"Listen, you two owl-hoots, and listen good. I want that horse back, and I want it back quick. I don't care how you do it, just get it back. Do I make myself clear?"

Silvertip bobbed his head up and down vigorously, while Blue John swallowed and nodded also, knowing he was looking into the blue barrel of death. Moore then released Silvertip, who stood up, straightened his shirt, and reached for the bag of gold.

"What do you think you are going to do with that gold?" Moore questioned ominously.

"Gee, Boss. You said to get the horse back, so I was just getting the money so's we could give it to the bishop when we took away his horse."

"*Give the money back?* By all the powers that be. . . !"

And Jack Moore was so angered that his face turned purple and he couldn't speak. Blue John, recognizing the symptoms of sudden death by lead poisoning, grabbed his bewildered partner, shoved him through the door and toward his horse, forked the saddle of his own bronc, and dusted his tail toward the narrow ford in the river.

Of one thing he was sure right then, and of one thing only. Without that blooded stud, his life and the life of Silvertip weren't worth the price of a plug of tobacco half-chewed.

Jack Moore, still trembling with anger, watched the two horse thieves swim their mounts across the river and finally disappear over the far rim in a cloud of dust.

Shaking his head once again in disbelief that Silvertip might actually have returned the money to the Mormon, Moore rose to his feet, picked up the heavy bag, set it atop a roof beam, and then strode through the door and down the trail toward his horse.

Suddenly and without warning an arm was thrown around Moore's neck and he was jerked violently backward, his breath shut off and his arms pinned to his sides. Instinctively he began to struggle, and then he felt the end of a pistol barrel pushing into his ribs. Without hesitation he ceased all movement and lifted his hands well above the pearl grips of his two famous pistols.

"All right, boys," a quiet voice ordered, "move in."

In a moment Moore found himself surrounded by several men, all heavily armed, all covered with a thick coat of trail dust, and all quite anxious, it appeared, to terminate his earthly existence.

Quickly his weapons were taken from him, and then a rope was taken from the nearest saddle. Moore, seeing that, spoke quickly.

"Who . . . who are you gents?"

"Well," the quiet man replied caustically, "we might be angels from heaven, only we ain't. We might be outlaws like you, only we ain't that, either. We might also be the law, but if we claimed that, it wouldn't be true. At least, not exactly. What we are, Mr. Whatever-your-name-is, is a posse from Cisco, the ones who lost their horse. We followed those two friends of yours, and got here just in time to see them disappear over the far rim. So, you'll have to do. Now where is our horse?"

"You followed those two idiots all the way here?"

"Right as rain. Say, but you think fast. Why, I'd be willing to lay a bet that you even know what we are going to do next, what the law says to do to any hombre who steals horses."

"Now, boys, don't be hasty. I didn't take your horse. I swear I didn't. It was Blue John and Silvertip who done it. They—"

"Hank, shake out your rope. I'm fixing to give this owl-hoot a hemp neck massage. I've heard that a stretched-out neck cures a whole lot of common ailments, such as lying and such."

"No!" Jack Moore shouted, pleading desperately now. "What I told you is true, so help me! Those two took your horse, but they sold it to some Mormon over in Sanpete. That's where they've gone now, to get it back."

"Sold it, huh? Well, that would explain why the prints disappeared, wouldn't it?"

"Yeah, that was why, I swear it!"

"Where's the money they got for it?"

"Beats me," Moore lied. "They wanted to get rid of it quick, so they sold it for fifty bucks or so and probably lost that gambling. That's why I was so sore and sent them back. I got nothing out of the deal.''

"Jules," the man with the quiet voice asked, "how much do you reckon that stud is worth?"

One of the men in the posse did some quick figuring and then replied: "Well, at least a thousand, maybe fifteen hundred dollars. It depends."

"Could a man tell by looking that the stallion was worth that much?"

"Well, I hope to shout he could! Have you seen the points of that animal? His eyes, his chest, his hips, his—''

"Thanks, Jules. Well, outlaw, fifty dollars, did you say? My, my, my. Hank, shake out that rope, and let's string him up.''

Moore watched with fearful intensity as the rope snaked up over a huge limb and dropped back to dangle near him. Casually the man took hold of the loop and drew it loose, then slipped it over Moore's head and tightened it about his neck.

"Hank, dally it up and take in the slack. When you're ready, slap your spurs, and—''

"No! Wait!''

"Yes?''

"I . . . well, ah, I reckon I'd better level with you boys. I mean, maybe Blue John and Silvertip got a little more than fifty dollars when they sold your horse.''

"How much more, son?''

"Put the rope away, let me go, and I'll tell you everything.''

"What do you think boys? Is he worth it?''

Jack Moore watched anxiously as each of the men considered and then nodded.

"Okay, outlaw, you tell us. If what you say is worthwhile, then we put up the rope and you ride away a free man. If it isn't. . . .''

Hastily Moore began talking, and in a few moments the posse had gone to the cabin and had the gold counted out on the table.

"Well, boys," the posse leader said, "eighteen hundred dollars gold, just like this feller said. I reckon now I'm ready to propose two things. The first is that we let this pilgrim go, provided that he goes east, that he goes in a hurry, and that he never returns. My second proposal is that we take this money, consider the horse sold, and go home. Jules, you put the value on the horse, and it was yours. Is this enough?''

''It sure is!''

''There it is, boys. Besides, it looks to me like that Mormon feller has enough troubles as it is, with those other two owl-hoots after him. He thinks he bought the critter fair and square, so if he can keep it, then I say let him. Are you ready to head back?''

There was a chorus of agreement, and in a few moments two clouds of dust left the secluded bottom of the Green River. Jack Moore, the Boss, was churning up the ground eastward, his holsters empty and his mind filled with all sorts of new resolutions. The posse were themselves headed west, thoughts of home on all of their minds. And to a man they were relieved that the stallion was sold and that they had gotten such a good price for it. Why, eighteen hundred dollars gold was a powerful lot of money! It surely was!

7

A Very Good Runner

In Aspen Wells during the summer of '88 there wasn't much more to do of a night than sit around counting crickets, swatting 'skeeters, and watching the nails rust in the barn door. What recreation there was, folks had to provide for themselves. Drama and theatre were popular, either with local groups or sometimes touring professional actors putting on the shows. Wrestling, Cornish style, was sure to draw a good crowd, as was racing. And dancing—well, folks surely did go for dancing.

Down in the middle of town we had what we called the Pavilion. It was a large log structure with a stage at one end and two big old potbellied stoves on either side. The Pavilion was where we held all the drama productions, and it was also where we held the dances. Summer and winter, folks danced there, no matter what the weather was like outside. On rainy nights mud would get tracked in, and once folks got to dancing the mud dried up and got stomped into dust which rose up so thick it liked to choke a body to death. And on cold nights those stoves would get red hot, and folks would dance in a half circle around those stoves, doing their best to keep at least one side warm.

So we had some fine dances, and even us fellers who didn't dance much enjoyed going just so we could watch the other folks acting foolish.

That was why when Pa announced at our monthly family meeting that there was going to be a dance the next night I got so excited. I simply liked to go. Yet there was another reason, and I reckon I ought to admit it. You see, I was hankering to see Ida Mae again, and I was fairly certain that she would be there.

Now, I'd been over to Aunt Polly's when Lyman and Jim were sprucing up for a dance, though I'd never really done any honest sprucing myself. Yet I'd watched and I was pretty certain that I could handle it. So the next night, as soon as I finished straining the milk, I headed for the loft where I slept. It was Saturday night, but I wasn't about to take time to drag out the wash tub and take a bath. I'll tell you what I did have time for, though, and that was Pa's straightedge razor. Now, Pa was over at Aunt Victoria's eating dinner, so for the first time in my life I began to lather up. To be right truthful I'm not sure that I actually needed a shave, but Jim had been giving me the raspberries about my fuzz for quite a while, so I figured the time was ripe.

Luckily for me, Ma had taken the egg basket down to the coop about the time that I needed to gather up the makings, so in no time I had stripped the washroom and was up in my loft whittling away like I had been born to it. And would you believe it? Nervous though I was, my first shave ended with not so much as the slightest mark on my face—well, except for maybe one tiny slash under my chin.

Now, on my way out to do the chores I had taken Pa's hair grease and stashed it in the ditch. I was sure Pa wouldn't mind my using it, but I didn't want to endure the chiding my younger sisters would throw at me if they saw me putting it on.

So I slipped outside, greased down my hair and my boots a bit, and then lit out. And as luck would have it, who should I meet as I rounded the house but Ma. I thought for sure I had been nabbed, but Ma just looked at me and beamed. Right then I was glad I had a face that at least a mother could love, for there was no mistaking how she looked at me. She cautioned me to be home by ten o'clock, and pointed out that staying out any longer would provide chances for nothing but no good.

I agreed and got away without her noticing that my cane wasn't along, and that was a relief. I headed over to the Big House to pick up Ernest, and Aunt Polly saddled us with our younger sister Martha, too. But that didn't bother us too much, for we could easily ditch her if we needed to.

As we approached the Pavilion I started getting uneasy, thinking about Ida Mae, and by the time we reached the door I was as nervous as a duck in the desert. Once inside, though, I got caught up in the excitement of it all and was able to relax. That is, I relaxed until I saw Ida Mae. There she was, all smiles and sweetness, dancing up a storm with that rotten Pete Livingston!

I hadn't forgotten the welt that had been raised on the back of my head by Pete's bosom buddy Curly, and knowing that those two were thicker'n bobcats in a gunny sack, I couldn't help but feel distrustful of both of them. But doing my best to appear calm and nonchalant I made a beeline for Ida Mae. I decided to rescue her in style, so I laid my hand on Livingston's shoulder, coughed a little, and said, "Excuse me, but could I have this dance?"

Right off I knew I had made a grave mistake. Pete Livingston merely swirled Ida Mae around so he was facing me, and then he blurted, "Well, if it isn't old Clubfoot Soderberg, hisself! What'cha want, Limpy Leg? Har Har Har!"

Well, I could feel the red creeping up my neck again, but I wasn't going to be put off that easy. So I said, "I would like a dance with Ida Mae, please. I'm cutting in."

"Why, you skinny sawed-off little cripple! You ain't big 'nuff to see over a sway-backed burro, let alone dance with a girl like Ida Mae. Now go sit down like a good little boy, and stop embarrassing the lady here."

Well, I was madder than a rained-on rooster, and I was all set to light into him, bigger than me or not, when he turned his back on me, swept Ida Mae into his arms, and twirled her away. And the look on her face stopped me cold. There she was, after seeing me humiliated, grinning up at that no-account tomcat like there was no other fellow on earth but him.

66

I stood there momentarily, feeling lower than a snake's belt buckle in a wagon rut, sincerely wishing that I was dead or maybe hadn't come to the dance. Then Ernest and some girl bumped into me, and I decided the best place for me was not in the middle of the floor. So I hobbled over to lean against the wall and nurse my wounds in private.

After a minute or so, though, I noticed Uncle Albert's beaver hat bobbing up and down in front of me in tune with the Virginia Reel. Now, that would have been fine, except that I happened to know that Uncle Albert was out at the herd, so whoever it was under that hat had to be someone other than Uncle Albert. I leaned a little closer so I could see past all the gray hair, and there on the back of that old geezer's ear was the exact same mole that graced the back of Pa's ear. By golly, Pa had come to the dance! And as if to confirm my thoughts, the old fellow turned around, grinned, and gave me a big wink. Well, it sure was Pa.

I reckon this is the time to explain that Pa was a natural-born actor, and was in as many drama productions as he dared to be in. His favorite role, the one he did best, was playing the part of an old man. Why, when he painted up his face, colored his whiskers, put on his wig, and changed his voice, a body would have sworn that he was older than Moses or one of those other biblical fellers. So there I was, grinning and watching Pa enjoy the dance, when I glanced at the door just in time to see Marshal Clawson saunter in.

Pa saw him, too, and for an instant he froze. All I could think was, "Oh no! Some dirty so-and-so has squealed on Pa!"

But then I saw Pa lean over and whisper to old Hans Weegin, who was sitting next to him. Hans got right up, walked over to the marshal, welcomed him to the dance, and then led him over to the chair he had vacated next to Pa.

Well, I about died. I thought Pa had lost his mind, and I set myself to jump on the marshal so Pa could get away. But Pa never moved a muscle to run. He just sat there, ignoring the marshal and tapping his feet to the music like he was having the time of his life.

That was the first time I'd seen Marshal Clawson up close, and it didn't take me long to realize that he wasn't much to look at. What hair he had was long and yellow, his clothes were dirtier than a squaw-man's blanket, and his boots were so frazzled he couldn't scratch a match without burning his feet. His most distinctive feature, however, was his nose, which was big enough to store a small dog in. In short, Deputy Clawson was uglier'n a fresh-foaled moose, which he mightily resembled. Add to that the fact that he had all the social graces of a used-up horseshoe, and you can see what we were up against.

When the fiddles finally stopped, Pa sat there for a moment watching the folks on the floor getting ready for the next set. Then he turned his head, and if I hadn't known better I would have sworn that was the first instant that Pa saw the marshal. Golly, but my Pa was an actor!

For a second or two Pa just stared at him, but then he grinned that warm old grin of his that could make a body feel like he'd just come in out of a blizzard. Extending his hand to shake the marshal's he introduced himself in a squeaky old voice that made him sound at least a hundred and eighty-three.

"Well, how-de-do, stranger," he squeaked. "Welcome to the dance!"

He then began pumping the deputy's hand up and down, up and down, just as vigorously as he could. He didn't let up, either. He just kept on shaking hands until Marshal Clawson finally got tired of it and jerked his hand free. Then with a muttered oath the marshal began massaging his fingers, which Pa had undoubtedly crushed in his vice-like grip.

"Right pert dance these youngsters are having here," Pa commented. The marshal nodded in agreement, still massaging his fingers and arm where Pa had about shaken it loose from its socket.

"Yer a-talking to Avery Goodrunner," Pa said seriously, and I could tell that old Hans Weegin, who was standing next to me against the wall, was about to bust open, he was trying so hard to keep from laughing. But the marshal never got the joke, it having floated somewhere over the top of his thinly planted yellow hair.

"Hebron Clawson," he said, almost reaching out to shake Pa's hand again. Pa reached out, too, but just in time Marshal Clawson jerked his own back, unconsciously massaging his fingers again. I reckon he recalled the shaking of a moment before, and was not exactly anxious for another go-around.

"You here to dance?" Pa asked suddenly.

"Well, no, not exactly. I'm here, well, I'm here on business."

"Humph! Must be a mighty fine business that would bring a man out to a shindig like this one is shaping up to be. Say, what might your business be?"

"Uh . . . well . . . uh. . . . Say, old man, have you lived here all your life?"

"Nope—leastwise not yet. Why?"

"Do you know the bishop? Soderberg, I think his name is?"

"Do I know the bishop? Well, I should smile I do. Him and his Daddy, too. And fine men they are, both of them. Honest, loyal, up-standing, humble, courageous—"

"Courageous!" the marshal shouted. "Soderberg? Why that mealy-mouthed yellow-backed. . . . Why, I've never seen a man with so much run in him. If I could be alone with him for two minutes, old man, then you'd see how courageous he is."

"My heavens, sir," Pa squeaked, "you can't be talking about Bishop Soderberg—*our* Bishop Soderberg! Big fellow, strong as an ox, mean as a catamount, handsome as a stage performer? Is that the man?"

"Big, maybe," the marshal replied. "Tall, heavy, pretty much run to blubber and fat, cowardly, and so on. That is about like I'd describe him."

Well, I could see the fire in Pa's eyes, the marshal talking about him that way. But Pa held it in well, he surely did.

"Say," Pa said, "if we're talking about the same man, you'd better not let him hear you talking like that."

"Why not? There ain't nothing he can do to me."

"Oh, I don't know," Pa squeaked. "Why, he might get riled and pull those long yellow mustaches right off. He might do just that."

So they sat there for a few more minutes while Pa commented over and over about the deputy's mustaches and what a fine honest face he had.

"You a Mormon, Clodson?" Pa asked suddenly.

"Clawson," the deputy replied.

"What do you mean, Clodson?" Pa asked, sounding awfully puzzled.

"I said, my name is Clawson!"

"What of it? I don't understand."

"Why, you called me Clodson."

"Why'd I do that?"

"Well," the deputy responded impatiently, "I guess you thought it was my name."

"What was?" Pa asked seriously, sounding downright dumbfounded. I don't know how Pa kept a straight face. I was grinning from ear to ear, and old Hans Weegin was about to bust a gasket.

"What was?" Pa asked again.

"Clodson!" the deputy replied with exasperation.

"But you just now said it was Clawson," Pa said. "And now you say Clodson. You've got me right confused."

"Well, it is. I was trying to—"

Pa then reached over and took the marshal's arm and pulled him close.

"Young man," he said, speaking sternly, "you have an honest face but it doesn't seem to go very deep. Straighten up now and listen to the wisdom of old age. If your name is Clawson, own up to it. Don't pretend that it's Clodson. A man who is shifty will never get anywhere here in the west, especially not here in Utah. It just doesn't fit a Utahite. Leave all such petty flim-flamming to Easterners like that rabble of oppressors and murderers of the righteous who go around with stars on their chests calling themselves marshals, and who, to a man, have incipient hoof-and-mouth disease. Yes, sir, if your name is Plodson, admit it like a man. Let your nay be nay and your yea be yea, and you'll get along much better here in Aspen Wells."

Well, Marshal Clawson was so flustered that he was turning purple, but Pa was giving him no chance to interrupt, no chance at all.

"Now, Mr. Plumson," Pa continued, his voice squeaking more than ever, "I don't recollect you ever stating your business."

"It's Clawson," the deputy fumed, "and—"

"Now hold on, son. How in the world can your name also be your business?"

"Listen, you old geezer!" the marshal shouted at Pa. "My name is Clawson and my business is United States deputy marshal, and—"

"Son," Pa said as he placed his hand on the deputy's arm again, "you've no need to shout. My age may be great but my hearing is still quite good. So you are a marshal, eh? My, my, my, and you did look like such an honest young man. Still, we all must do *something* for a livelihood. Isn't that true?

"Folks," Pa suddenly squealed, pulling himself to his feet where he stood tottering back and forth, "this here stranger in our midst is Deputy Marshal Clodson, and he has been kind enough to come to our shindig tonight just to be neighborly. Now, he hasn't come right out and said so, but I reckon he'd be plumb tickled if he was to catch himself a polygamist, as I take that to be his main line of work. Neighbors, he seems especially interested in our bishop, so if any of you know of that good man's whereabouts, Plodson here would surely appreciate hearing from you. Now, don't be bashful. Step right up and—"

At that moment a funny thing happened. Pa almost toppled over, saving himself only by reaching out as he fell and latching onto the long drooping mustaches of Marshal Clawson. That worthy let out a yell like he'd been scalped (which he probably felt like he had), pushed Pa off of him, stuttered and stammered for a moment while he made sure that his mustaches were still part of his anatomy, and then he turned with an oath and stalked out the door. A moment later we all heard the pounding of hooves as one deputy marshal, once again minus his dignity, departed the vicinity. That man was getting right irked at my Pa.

For a moment there was total silence, and then old Hans Weegin held up a mug of cider from the refreshment table and shouted, "Brothers and sisters, ladies and gentlemen, a toast. To all federal marshals and other minions of the law: may they be winked at by blind men, kicked cross lots by cripples, nibbled to death by ducks, and carried to hell through the keyhole by bumblebees."

There was a roar of laughter, and I could see that Pa had won another round.

8

The Seeds of Opposition

Pa's performance that night beat all I'd ever seen, and most folks there were having a right good chuckle. But then Mungus Sorenson put a sudden damper on things when he and George "Loose-lip" Lundstrom swaggered over and knocked both wig and hat off of Pa's head.

Then Loose-lip, living up to his reputation as a loudmouth, spit a mouthful of black tobacco juice right on Pa's boot. Wiping the drizzle from his whiskers with his shirt sleeve, he grinned and spoke.

"Well, well," he said, "beneath the disguise of an old idiot we find an honest-to-goodness real one."

Instantly the crowd grew silent, and Loose-lip, a little awed at his own bravery, hastily retreated behind Mungus, where he stood looking like he expected at any moment to have the roof fall in on him.

"Well, bishop," Mungus sneered, "you got lucky again. I'm amazed that one of these fine upstanding citizens didn't turn you in. Had I been any closer I would have, but no matter. Sooner or later Clawson will get you." He paused, then added: "Say, how's that old nag of yours doing? Somebody said you'd been out racing him with the tithing chickens.''

Two or three people laughed, and Mungus, sensing sympathy from the crowd, boldly continued.

''Now, lookey here, folks. What we've got here is a bishop who is not only stupid but is likely dishonest as well. He sits right here and plays idiot right in front of the marshal, laughing at the danger of it, with never so much as a thought about who'd take care of his family or the ward if he was to get captured. Besides that, he boasts of going out and giving a full eighteen hundred dollars for a plug, and no bishop I ever heard of has that kind of money, especially to spend on a worthless plug. Now I ain't accusing, but I am wondering if our good bishop has been dipping into the tithing funds without us knowing of it.''

Now, I'd been around Pa when he was mad plenty of times, but I'd never seen him come so close to boiling over and still manage to keep his lid on. And all I could think of was what Pa kept telling us youngsters over and over again, that we ought to be actors rather than reactors. In short, we ought to be our own men. Pa called it succumbing to social pressure, and right then he was surely showing all of us how to resist it. If I ever saw social pressure I saw it that night at the dance.

''He tells us,'' Mungus continued, ''that he paid that much for the stud so he could keep out of reach of the marshals. He tells us that nag is fast, and he tells us that he bought it from two strangers down near Ephraim. Now, I don't know about any strangers, as no one has seen them before or since, and that seems right incriminating to me. But I do know horses, and there was never a plug born that was good for racing, or for being worth the handsome sum of eighteen hundred dollars gold. That I do know!

''Soderberg, I say that you are either an idiot or a fraud, and my guess would be that you are both. To my way of thinking, there are only two ways that you can prove otherwise. First, submit to an audit of the tithing office and storehouse. Second, race that fool horse and prove to us that it can run. Right frankly, I'm personally willing to bet five twenty-dollar gold pieces that you're too yellow to do either.''

"Yeah, Soderberg," echoed Loose-lip. "And I'm willing to go Mungus here one better. I'll not only bet a hundred dollars that you won't take the challenge, but I'll bet another hundred that your old nag couldn't make it from here to Salt Lake City in a whole week."

"Now, hold up," Hans Weegin said, pushing himself forward. "You boys are taking advantage of this here situation. You know as well as I do that Soderberg here is the bishop, and that means he ain't allowed to bet. You know that bishops don't gamble or do none of them other hell-raising things, so how come you're trying to force him into doing something that he hadn't ought to?"

"Shut up, Weegin," Mungus snapped, "before you get thrown out of here on your ear. What's it going to be, Soderberg? Put up or shut up?"

Pa was so angry that I think I could see smoke coming out of his ears, and just when I expected him to snap Mungus in two, bishop or no, Ma stepped forward. Smiling sweetly, she took Pa's arm in a persuasive manner and said, "Jons, have you ever noticed how the scum rises when the pot boils?"

Still smiling then, she led Pa toward the center of the floor.

"What do you say, Jons?" she asked. "Don't you think we're all about ready for another Virginia Reel?"

I guess those boys in the band were fearful of the dance ending, for the music was going quicker than a tie comes off after meeting. As for me, I went back to my corner where I could get the heat off and take a breather. What a terrible night! Ida Mae had disgraced me, her father had disgraced Pa, and what could we do about it? As far as I could tell, nothing!

When I got home Ma was there, and she asked me to go up and say prayers with my little sister. I did, and I thought it was pretty special when she prayed for Pa, asking Heavenly Father to help him resist all his social pressure. The way it sounded, Ma had read the situation about like I had.

Later, long after I should have been asleep, I heard Pa come in the back way. Ma, who was downstairs churning cream, stopped immediately. There was a long silence, and then Pa asked Ma if he could spend the night. Now, you would be interested in knowing that although Ma was Pa's third wife, when Pa had serious problems he usually came to our home. I don't know why, unless it was because Ma could tell Pa he was either right or wrong in the nicest way a body ever heard.

"Hey, Pa," I grinned, leaning out over the loft, thinking to tease him like he was always teasing me. "Old Mungus sure got to you tonight, didn't he? What are you going to do now, go after him with—"

"Hyrum Soderberg," Pa shouted angrily, "be still and get to bed! Your bad manners ill become who you are, young man. To help you learn that lesson, you will consider yourself barred from all outside activities for one month! Do I make myself clear?"

Embarrassed and humiliated, I nodded and withdrew to my bed. Good grief! What had brought that on? I wondered. Pa was suddenly as touchy as a blistered heel. A month! For crying out loud, that was a long time. Especially was it a long time when I was only teasing him. Scrud! When he teased me I was supposed to laugh and take it. If I could, why couldn't he? Sometimes parents are surely difficult to understand.

After a little while he and Ma started talking about what had happened at the dance, and it was easy to tell that Pa was upset, maybe more upset than I had ever seen him. Over the years Mungus had given Pa plenty of cause for grief, but this was the first time Pa had ever let it bother him. Up to then the fact that he was the bishop had always cooled him down, but that night it made no difference, no difference at all. Pa even ignored Ma when she reminded him of who he was.

Apparently several people had echoed Mungus's doubts, some about his money and others about the speed of his horse, and that really hurt Pa. He had always been a stickler for honesty, and more than any man I knew he had made it a policy of going the extra mile. One time some butter spoiled in the storehouse, and Pa replaced it with some of our own, saying that the Lord always blessed those who gave freely, even and maybe especially when they weren't obligated to give. So it wounded him deeply when folks began questioning his honesty. It also hurt him to have folks questioning his judgment regarding the speed of his horse, especially when he was so convinced that he was right.

Ma, sensing Pa's real problem, repeated to Pa his own favorite lecture, the one he gave to me whenever someone made me feel bad about being crippled—the lecture about not letting social pressure pull me down.

"Hyrum," he would say, putting his hands on my shoulders, "does it really matter what other people say or do? Not really, not when you understand that God never makes mistakes. Certainly he made you different, but that was not an accident. He's given you special blessings to compensate for your club foot, and he's left the realization of those blessings up to you. Now, you can either spend your time happily enjoying the discovery of them, or you can waste your days wallowing in the mire of self-pity. Hyrum, people are a lot like chickens. If one is different, no matter why, most of the others will mercilessly peck it to death. When you reach the point where you are unaffected by the silly surface peckings of social pressure, only then will you approach the potential God has given you. And only then will you be truly happy."

Now Ma was using that same logic on Pa, pointing out that God had made him different by trusting him to be bishop. If he stooped as low as Mungus and Loose-lip wanted him to stoop, then he would be betraying God's trust and giving in to social pressure. Mungus and the others were just being normal chickens, she said, so it was up to Pa to rise above the flock and meet the potential God had given him.

Well, it tickled me to hear Ma talk to Pa like that, but it only made him more sore.

"Hattie," he said, "this is different, and you know it! A man does what he must! They've questioned my integrity, my judgment, and my honor. I am bound to protect my honor!"

"Jons," Ma said quietly, "your honor is unscathed. When a fly bites a horse, that doesn't change anything. The horse may flinch a bit, but it is still a horse, and the fly is still a fly. Your honor is as sound as ever. What has really been wounded is your pride."

"Honor!" declared Pa.

"Pride," Ma said gently.

"Honor!" Pa thundered, and right then I pulled my pillow over my head and went to sleep. After all, enough was enough, and I could tell that there would be little else said that night that was worth my remaining awake to hear.

I was still feeling sorry for myself the next morning, licking my wounds about being restricted and not being able to do anything with Ida Mae, when Pa hollered up at me to get about the chores. Then the door slammed, and I knew Pa was on his way to bishop's meeting. Well, it was all I could do to take leave of that feather mattress and drag myself down to the barn. I felt about as limp as a neck-wrung rooster. To me there never was any justice in having to do chores on the Sabbath. To my way of thinking, if the Lord had really wanted the day kept holy he would have had cows stop making milk every seven days, and so on. But he didn't, so I had the milking to do.

Anyway, I finished up and hitched the team just in time for Ma and all the little girls to clamber aboard. "Let's go, Hyrum," she called, trying to get me to hurry with getting the cow-smell off my hands. "We're late! Why, if we should ever walk into that meeting before your father gets up to start it, I expect he would faint on the spot."

Sure enough, we were late again, but there was a pew up front that was empty as could be, and for that we headed. To tell the truth, I quite enjoyed sitting next to my little sisters, as it made me feel important helping Ma while Pa sat up front. The only thing bad about it was hobbling all the way to the front while folks looked at us.

We settled ourselves just as the opening hymn was ending, and out of habit I turned and glanced around to see where Jim, Lyman, and Ernest were sitting. Little did I expect to see, directly behind me, Ida Mae. Not only was I stunned that she would be there so close to me, but I was shocked to see her father, Mungus, sitting next to her. What in blazes is he doing here? I wondered, slowly working my neck back into its socket. Impulsively I glanced up to where Pa was sitting, and, sure enough, there he was, looking right through me. And he was wearing that little smile, too, the one that always meant he was about to do something unexpected. And I didn't have long to wait to find out what, either, for right after the opening prayer Pa rose to his feet and began to speak. I don't recollect all he said, but a good portion of it I'm fairly sure I will never forget.

"Brothers and sisters," he boomed, "welcome to meeting. Welcome especially to those of you who have not made a habit of attending. It's always a pleasure to see the sinner cast off his yoke of bondage and return to the fold."

Pa grinned at Mungus as he said that, and then he continued.

"Since the dance last night, I've done considerable thinking about the subject for this morning's sermon. I'd like to take my text from Proverbs, chapter 16, verse 27, which says, 'An ungodly man diggeth up evil, and in his lips there is as a burning fire.' Now, last night at the dance the whole ward saw a classic example of this scripture. There were those who sought to dig up evil and spread the fiery words of falsehood, and they did their very best to discredit your bishop and undermine his effectiveness.

"Brothers and sisters, I will be the first to admit to mortal weaknesses, and very likely I have many more than a man in my position ought to have. But a liar I am not, a thief I am not, and a coward I am not! All of these accusations were either implied or stated explicitly. As a man of honor I feel duty bound to dispel these falsehoods and lay to waste the weeds of wickedness and deceit which even now are beginning to choke out the simple stems of truth which ought to flourish in Aspen Wells.

"Therefore, after a sleepless night of considering all the alternatives, I have determined to accept the challenge so offensively thrown at me. I will cover the bets made by Brothers Sorenson and Lundstrom. Furthermore, to show my contempt of them and all others who are making wind with such wild accusations, I will extend my bet to any and every other gentleman who might feel inclined to doubt the speed and stamina of my stallion, Ingersol. I will place one hundred dollars in gold against each of you who wishes to bet an equal amount. My bet is that I can ride that Belgian stallion which I have named Ingersol from the gate of our cemetery to the Temple block in Salt Lake City between sunup and sundown of this coming Wednesday.

"Any and all takers are welcome to meet me on the front steps immediately following the meeting, as such business ought not to be conducted within the Lord's house.''

Well, you should have heard the sisters gasp. Ma was fit to be tied, and Aunt Polly and Aunt Victoria, Pa's other two wives, were just as upset. I could tell that no matter where Pa spent that night, he would be in a world of hurt.

After the meeting there must have been at least three dozen men take up Pa's bet, and at least as many more wanted to, but weren't allowed to by their wives, I guess. Mungus and Loose-lip were, of course, first in line, and as they walked away I saw Mungus poke Loose-lip in the ribs and grin, saying, ''We done it. That's the end of Soderberg. Shake hands with the man who will be your new bishop.''

At the moment I didn't understand what he meant, and as I rode home in the wagon with Ma I worried about it. But I didn't worry about that nearly so much as I worried about where Pa was going to get three thousand six hundred dollars gold. Goes to show how shortsighted a fellow can be.

9

Outlaws Within and Without

On Devil's Lookout, a rocky outcropping high in the hills above Aspen Wells, the outlaw known as Blue John sat in the sparse shade of a juniper, better known locally as a cedar tree, waiting impatiently for the return of his twice-slow partner, Silvertip.

Down the steep slope a flock of magpies screamed their displeasure at the world, two or three flies were doing their best to share the limited shade with the outlaw's wildly swinging sombrero, and now and then a welcome breeze whispered through the cedar boughs above. Other than that there was no sound but the heavy scrambling of hooves on rocks as Silvertip's three horses laboriously climbed the hill below.

For thirty minutes Blue John had watched his partner approaching, and now as Silvertip drew near he could see that the man was coated with dust. Wistfully he realized that he looked the same, that both of them smelled of horses, leather, and stale sweat, and that down in Aspen Wells the barbershop had a tub and some warm water which could be his for only two bits an hour.

"Ah, well," he mumbled, "that tub might just as well be in San Francisco for all the good it will do me."

At last Silvertip pulled up, the two horses he was leading snorting and blowing behind him.

He sat for a moment, wiping his face with his bandana. Then he spat in the dust and spoke.

"Sure is hot," he said.

"Yeah," replied Blue John, "and dry enough to make the bushes follow the dogs around. Did ya bring the water?"

"Yup. Here, have a drink."

"I see, Silvertip, that you have two fine broomtails there. That's wonderful, but you went after the stallion. Where's it at?"

"Well, you see, Blue John, I seen that stallion all right, but I have no earthly idea how we're going to get him."

"Why not? We'll get him just like we did the last time. That bishop can't be any harder to steal from than those folks were down at Cisco."

"No, I reckon it'd be easy to steal that nag from the bishop, but stealing it from the whole town is not so easy, and I ain't so sure I want to try it now."

"What are you talking about, Silvertip?"

"I don't know, Blue John. Something funny is going on down there, and I sure don't know what to make of it. They have our plug, all right, but half of the men in town are guarding him with rifles."

"What? Do they suspect us?"

"Naw, nothing like that. As far as they are concerned, we don't even exist."

"Then why, blast it? Why are they guarding our stud?"

"Why, I know it sounds plumb crazy, but word is that tomorrow there is going to be a big race, and that bishop we sold the horse to is going to race that same plug in it."

"Aw, come on, Silvertip. You know that nag ain't no race horse."

"I know it, and you know it, too. But honest, Blue John, that's what they told me was coming off. Funny thing is, most of them fellers down there don't think he can race, either. That's why they're guarding him so closely. They don't want the bishop switching horses or doing something so's the horse can't race."

"Whatsa matter? Don't they trust him?"

"I don't reckon, Blue John. Not when so many of 'em have a hundred dollars gold bet against him."

"Whewee! A hundred dollars each? Does the bishop have that kind of money?"

"Beats me," Silvertip said, shaking his head. "But those folks seem to think he does. They trust him that far, at least. Anyhow, bad as the Boss wants that horse back, I don't reckon we'll get him until after the race."

"Who's he racing against?"

"Nobody. He's racing against time. He's got to get from here to Salt Lake between sunup and sundown tomorrow."

"Why, shucks, that's a hundred and ten miles! I say it can't be done."

"Blue John, you sound like them folks down there. Maybe you want to ride on down and place a bet, along with them folks, against the bishop? Let me tell you, there ain't many horses that could survive a one-day trip that long. I had one once that might have done it. Best horse I ever had. But that Belgian? I doubt it. He's big and he's strong, but I don't think he's that strong. And that bishop ain't no little man, either. He'll wear out that nag in a hurry. Way I see it, those folks are about to make themselves an easy hundred bucks."

"You're right, Silvertip. And the way I see it, it's our job to guarantee that the citizens down there win. Did you learn his route?"

"Yeah, sure. A fellow by the name of Sorenson told me there was only one way he could go, and that was over through Salt Creek Canyon, past Nephi, and then straight as the crow flies past Provo, through the Jordan Narrows, and into Salt Lake Valley. But Blue John, how we going to guarantee that the bishop loses?"

"Silvertip, I reckon the Boss is right. In some ways you're awful shy of smarts. We're after that horse, ain't we? And after they start the race, he won't be guarded, will he? So all we have to do is drift on up the canyon a few miles, drop down on him when he goes past, and the horse is ours."

"Gee, Blue John, don'tcha feel kinda sorry for the bishop, him losing twice, the horse and the money, like he'll be doing?"

"Oh, for—! Silvertip, how in blazes did you ever become an outlaw? Now, come on, let's get riding. We've got to find an ambush site before dark. By the way, these are awful pretty mares. Matched white, ain't they? I reckon we can play our own out, if need be, and then switch to these white critters you picked up, as we chase down the bishop. We'll bushwhack him before he even sees us, and even if he does see two riders bearing down on him, he'll see these white mares and think we're his neighbors. Why, this is going to be easy as whistling."

"Gee, Blue John. How'd you ever think of such a good plan? I wish I could think of plans like that!"

"Oh, it weren't nothing. Now, come on, let's ride!"

Earlier that day, in a back room of the Aspen Wells Co-op, Mungus Sorenson and several of the more-than-eager-to-grow-financially men of the town sat in animated conversation.

"Boys," Mungus was saying, "I tell you, it's in the bag! By sundown tomorrow Soderberg will be in the Territorial prison, and we'll have won the bets and collected by default. Everything he owns, including the dairy pasture and that fine brick home, will be ours, and Aspen Wells will be needing a new bishop. The choice is obvious, and yours truly will be ready to accept."

"But, Mungus," questioned Jesse Christensen, "what if Soderberg should win? How do we know he's going to get arrested?"

"Why, that's easy," sneered Mungus. "We've set him up, and since you boys will be helping me, I see no reason why I shouldn't lay it all out for you. Less than an hour from now, Loose-lip will leave for Nephi on the train. Once there, he will telegraph Territorial Marshal Dyer in Salt Lake City, telling him of Soderberg's route through the Jordan Narrows and into the city. By the time the bishop gets past Porter Rockwell's old saloon and into the narrows, there will be twenty to thirty deputies swarming over him like bees over honey. He won't stand a chance of ever seeing the city, let alone reaching the Temple block.

"Now, before he gets to those narrows we'll do everything in our power to slow him down. That's just in case the marshals don't make it or he slips through them. So far that man has been shot with luck, but I suspect this will end it. Tonight my son Curly and the Livingston kid will sneak into Soderberg's tack room, put cockleburs under his saddle blanket, and cut his cinch-strap nearly in two. That's just for starters.

"Pain, before daylight tomorrow I want you up on the Divide starting a bunch of fires in that cheat grass. All that fire and smoke will at the very least affect the stallion's breathing, and it might even spook it clear out of the country. Jesse, you take Anson Holman and Ollie Johnson here, and hightail it up the canyon to the Petticoat Cliffs. You three will be outlaws, so disguise yourselves well. Then when Soderberg crosses Salt Creek, stick him up. Take your time and go through everything he's got, dump his canteen, strip off his saddle, and if the cinch-strap hasn't broken yet, break it. Point is, your job is to cost Soderberg thirty minutes, and hopefully more.

"Scar, you take the train to Nephi with Loose-lip, steal a herd of cattle or sheep, drive 'em into the mouth of the canyon, and hold 'em there where the sides are so steep that a horse can't climb out of it. A good riled-up herd should cost him fifteen minutes, and, boys, every fifteen minutes counts!"

"Mungus," Jesse said in amazement, "you've sure thought of everything."

"Sure as sow bugs under a buffalo chip, Jesse. And there's one more thing that I haven't even told you. I have a lady friend up Santa-quin way, a lady friend who's agreed, for a certain . . . er . . . sum to be on the trail when the bishop rides past."

"Hey, she don't sound like much of a lady to me," Jesse said.

"So what?" questioned Scar. "Mungus, what's she gonna do there?"

"Why, Scar, I'm truly amazed! Everybody knows that a polyg loves women. Especially this polyg! She's a winsome lass, and she'll be lying near the trail with more troubles than old lady Lavine. When Soderberg stops to give the lady assistance, she'll occupy another half hour, and if it works out she'll bring him more grief than he ever thought possible. Can you imagine what a torn blouse and a scream would do to that man? Especially if some properly enraged citizens were hidden close by?''

"Why, hang it all!" breathed Scar. "That poor galoot don't stand a chance."

"He sure doesn't," agreed Ollie Johnson. "Why, it'd take an angel from heaven to get Soderberg past all that and into Salt Lake before sundown."

"Yeah," laughed Mungus. "It would take at least one and more than likely it would take a whole cloudful of 'em to get him through. And, boys, we all know he ain't got that kind of influence. Now when—"

Suddenly the door burst open and in staggered Curly, all out of breath from running.

"Pa," he gasped, "they're gone! Somebody stole the white mares, and they're gone!"

"What? How do you know they've not just strayed off?"

"Because Angie Holman saw some feller on a dark horse leading them up into the cedars. She said he was a big man—looked kinda like the bishop."

"Well, I'll be . . ." Mungus mumbled. "Boys, now those marshals will get the bishop for polygamy *and* horse-stealing. And, boys, that's not just prison, that's a hanging crime! Loose-lip, when you send that telegram, don't forget to tell Marshal Dyer that Soderberg has stolen our two white mares. Knowing what a coward the bishop is, he'll probably have two of those boys of his riding along on those mares as guards. He's got neither the guts nor the horses to tackle that race alone. I tell you, boys, Soderberg is as yellow as mustard without the bite! Now, let's get going. We've a lot to do before morning."

10

The Race Begins

It couldn't have been much later than three in the morning when I was awakened by the sound of tiny pebbles striking against my window pane. It took a minute for me to get my bearings, and then I staggered to the window to see who was causing all the fuss. It would have been like my brother Johnny to do a thing like that, but as far as I knew he was out at the herd. Still, you can imagine my surprise when I parted the curtains and saw Ida Mae standing in the moonlight, beckoning me to come down.

For about a millionth of a second I wondered if this was one of the activities Pa had restricted me from. But then I was dressed and out that window quicker than holly-be-scat. When I hit the ground right next to Ida Mae my heart was really pounding, and I was trying to think of something to say when she grabbed my arm and began pulling me toward the barn.

"Hurry," she whispered, "and don't talk. I've got a lot to tell you, and no time to tell it in. If Father checked my room we'd be in a whole lot more trouble than we are now."

By then we were inside the barn, and right off Ida Mae started crying. I'll tell you, there is nothing more discombobulating than to be with a girl when she starts crying. However, I at least had the sense to put my arms around her while she dried her tears, and that was a little slice of heaven for sure.

"Hy," she sobbed, "I don't even know exactly why I'm here. I love my father. He's a good man. I swear he is. It's just that he's so jealous, and . . . well, I just can't stand by and let him destroy himself by ruining another man."

"Ida Mae, what are you talking about?"

"Oh, Hyrum," she groaned, "don't you know? Father thinks your father stole his two white mares, and he's out to get him. Why, not more than an hour ago Curly and that mean old Pete Livingston accidentally woke me, bragging to Father about how they'd hid cockleburs under your father's saddle blanket, and I don't know what all else. Hyrum, what I ever saw in that Pete Livingston I'll never know. So please forgive me for the way I acted at the dance."

Well, she about had to scrape me off the rafters, I was floating so high. I wanted to dance and shout, but instead I mumbled, "Sure," and let it go at that. If I'd said much else I'd have been singing, and I can't carry a tune in a bucket.

"Cockleburs," I said, placing my feet firmly back into the issue. "Well, let's check out Pa's blanket."

Quickly I led the way into the tack room, lit the lantern, and pulled Pa's saddle blanket off the post. And Ida Mae was right. There, carefully buried in the fabric of that blanket, were nearly two dozen spiny cockleburs. I could see that it was going to be a job getting those burrs out, so I walked Ida Mae home, pulling the burrs out as we went. And despite the lateness of the hour I don't think I ever enjoyed a walk more.

She didn't try kissing me that night, which was a relief in several ways. I'd worried some about kissing, especially since Pa's talk with me, and it wasn't long before we got to talking about it.

Hardly had I mentioned kissing when Ida Mae apologized for pushing herself at me the way she had done. Without waiting for me to reply, she began talking about how her Ma had died some six years before, and how she missed having someone who could teach her the social graces, as she called them. That made me think of the things that Ma and Pa were always telling me, so I shared them with her.

Kissing, Ma said, was fun and exciting, but even more it was meant to express feelings of love and closeness. For that reason, it ought to be kept sacred, reserved only for the most special people. According to Ma, I said, kissing was a proper and special way of showing strong affection. But Ma said that if young people kissed too often they would soon tire of it and start looking for other ways to satisfy their emotions.

I then told her about the time when Pa sat all us boys down on a log up in Meetinghouse Canyon, where we were dragging out Lyman's first buck.

"Boys," he said, "a lot of young men acquire habits like that buck right there. They think life is simply for frolicking and for mating, and all young girls are seen as free game. They don't understand that Heavenly Father made mankind to be different, to be above the animals. While we do have some very strong and constant feelings, we are also told that we must learn to control them until we are married."

Pa then told us that before we could really love a young lady we first had to learn to trust and respect not only her but ourselves as well. That self-respect could only come by consistently practicing self-control. He then promised us that if we would always remember our priesthood, and honor it by controlling our actions, then we would never find ourselves mistaking lust for love. Love, he told us, gets crowded right out of a young relationship once a couple begin to focus on kissing and the like.

Pa then did something I'll never forget. Right there in the shadow of a huge pine he placed his hands on each of our heads and gave us a father's blessing, promising us by the power of his priesthood that we would have the strength to be true men as we prepared for our missions and for marriage in the temple.

"You know, Ida Mae," I said, "the other thing I will never forget was when Pa finished the blessings and stepped back onto a large rock there in the ravine. With tears in his eyes he told us how happy he had been each time he rode away from the Endowment House in Salt Lake City with each of our mothers as his new wives.

He said that those three days had been the most meaningful days of his life, and that we could enjoy the same eternal blessings and the same special feelings if we made up our minds right then to bridle our passions and to help the girls we were with to bridle theirs.''

"Hyrum," Ida Mae said, "you are so fortunate to have parents who are willing to share their wisdom with you. Mother would have, if she were only here. Father . . . well, he doesn't have time to think about it, and I'm afraid to ask him. Do you know why I kissed you that night after conjoint session? My girlfriends told me that boys like kissing, and I thought if you liked kissing, and if I kissed you, then you'd like me. And, Hyrum, I really wanted you to like me.''

Well, I just shrugged and kicked at a rock, because I surely didn't have anything to say to that, not anything at all.

"You know, Hyrum, maybe I shouldn't tell you this, but I've kissed a couple of other boys, too. I did it because I wanted in the worst way to be popular. Now, as I think of what your parents have told you, I can see that my girlfriends are not really popular at all. They're just available.''

"That's right, Ida Mae. Boys generally don't respect girls like that. They just use them. Too many kids think that to be popular they have to go along with the crowd, and do what everybody else is doing. Shucks, I've listened to Jim and Johnnie for years, and they both have some real stories to tell. But do you know what, Ida Mae? The girls they really like, the ones they take to church or bring home for all of us to meet, are not the ones you would call 'popular.'

"I asked our herder one time, after I'd seen him smooching with that Smith girl, if he was going to marry her. He laughed and told me no, that he just used her when he wanted a good time. He said that when he got married it would be to a girl he could respect. Ida Mae, I've never forgotten that. The thing that struck me as funny was that old Jake felt like he could mess around and do whatever he had a mind to do, and yet he would only marry a girl who had never done such things. Seems to me that the good Lord gave out rules for boys the same as for girls. I know my Pa sure doesn't believe there ought to be a double standard.''

As we approached her house she suddenly grinned, and looking over at me she spoke. "You know, Hyrum, I've been thinking that perhaps Father has been teaching me some good values after all. Just last week I heard him yelling at Curly, and he told him that kids who were fooling around where they hadn't ought to be would have more troubles than the little worm who accidentally crawled into a convention of hungry robins."

We both laughed, and then I watched from out in the road while she crawled into her window. I'll tell you, that Ida Mae was really something!

I was just getting back through my own window when I heard the folks stirring downstairs, and I hadn't even got the covers pulled over me when Ma called me softly to come down for breakfast.

"Pa," I asked as we were eating, "do you know anything about Mungus's white mares?"

"Nope. Nothing more than that they are certainly fine animals. Why do you ask?"

"Oh, no reason. I was just wondering. Pa, I found some burrs in your saddle blanket last night. Looked to me like somebody had put them there on purpose. Be careful, Pa. I just know somebody's after you."

"Hy," Pa answered, "there's a lot more than one person who'd like to see me lose today. Fact is, I wish there was some way out of this race. That was a foolish thing I did, letting myself be pushed into a corner by Mungus and his crowd. Trouble is, I'm here now, and the only way out is by riding north. Hyrum, your mother was right when she said I was being blinded by social pressure. The minute I gave in, that very minute, I lost control over my actions. Today I am not my own man."

As the sky started to gray in the east, the brethren who had been guarding Ingersol brought him to the barn, gave him a bag full of oats, and saddled him up. And none of them saw the cut in the cinch-strap that Curly had made. Anyway, after it was saddled Pa took the reins and together we walked through town and out to the cemetery.

I'd never seen so many folks assembled in Aspen Wells at one time. That is, not unless you count the time those two dancing bears got to fighting down behind the Pavilion. If we had been holding a meeting, that crowd would have set an attendance record.

Old Hans Weegin, one of those who had been guarding Pa's horse, placed his hand on Pa's arm and spoke.

"Bishop," he said, "it's a long way to Salt Lake City. A lot can happen to a man or his horse in a hundred and ten miles. My advice is to ride for your life and don't slow down for nothing or nobody. Use that horse wisely, and if you get all the breaks you might just make it."

As Pa started to climb into the saddle his foot slipped out of the stirrup, he about fell, and the crowd gave him a good hurrah. Stiffly then, and awfully embarrassed, Pa climbed aboard, doing his best to ignore the crowd as he smiled bravely at each of his wives. He knew he was heading for trouble, but he was game to go, just the same. I'll tell you, right then I loved my Pa so much that I could have popped my buttons. And it didn't matter whether or not he'd restricted me either. He was still a great man!

Just then I caught sight of Curly and Pete Livingston, and they were both as expectant as two robins watching a wormhole. Well, I grinned and winked at Pa, and he winked back, knowing exactly what I was tickled about. It's funny how disappointed a person is when something he's planned so carefully fails to come off, especially if it's supposed to be funny and is in reality a dirty trick. Shucks! I almost felt sorry for Curly, he looked so sour.

At that moment the first rays of the sun splashed across Pa's hat, and with a loud warwhoop he slapped the spurs to Ingersol and off he went. We all stood around and watched until even the dust vanished, and then as if on command the whole town turned and headed home.

11

Tucker Bill and the Crawler

We had just finished asking a blessing on my sisters' morning mush—something it dearly needed, in my opinion—when somebody started banging on the door. Since I'd already eaten I told Ma I'd answer it. As the door swung open I caught my breath in surprise, for there was Ida Mae again, so worked up and worried that I knew something else had gone drastically wrong.

Not waiting for greetings, she grabbed my arm and tugged, at the same time pulling the door shut behind me. "Oh, Hyrum," she gasped, trying to catch her breath, "Father has really done it now! I just heard him talking to another man about your father, and about some lady up at the Santaquin depot. She is going to stage a fake accident up on the hill south of the feed store in Santaquin. Father said she will be lying there in agony and pain as your father approaches. He also said something about her tearing her blouse and screaming, and that would get your father in real trouble! Hyrum, I don't know what got into Father, but I'm scared."

For a moment I stood there, shocked into silence. This was pretty bad, but what could I do? I'd seen Ingersol run, and I knew we had no horse that could hope to catch him now, not after a thirty-minute start. Neither could I send a telegram, for Pa would stay as far away from people and depots as he could. Wildly my mind searched, groping and grasping for an idea, but there was nothing, nothing at all.

"Ida Mae," I said at last, defeated, "I reckon I can't thank you enough for your concern. Sad thing is, there is nothing we can do now. Pa will just have to—"

And that was when I heard the train whistling, up at the depot. For a split second nothing registered, but then my mind reached out and took a-hold of that lonesome whistle, and a glimmer of hope leaped into my heart.

"Come on," I shouted, pulling Ida Mae off the porch after me. "We've got to get to the depot, and fast!"

There was no time to get one of our horses, but as we sprinted up the dusty road, here came Sister Dunn in her shiny new surrey. Not thinking of manners, I grabbed the reins and pulled her to a stop. Almost before I knew what I was doing, I was settling onto the seat next to Sister Dunn, and Ida Mae had climbed in on the other side of the surprised woman.

"Now see here, you—"

"Excuse me," I shouted, grabbing the reins, "but this is official Church business, Sister Dunn. We're working to save the bishop, and we need to get to the depot fast. Giddap, horse! Hyyahh!"

Well, that old horse did the double-shuffle for about five seconds, and then it took off like a shot-gunned rooster. I was clinging to those reins for all I was worth, and once when I happened to glance at Ida Mae I was surprised to see that she and Sister Dunn were holding on to each other like each was the rock of salvation. Not only that, but both of them had their mouths open and were scooping up flies like they'd missed their last meal. Simply put, they looked scared. But then I probably did, too, though I couldn't see myself too well. Truth was, I'd never driven a buggy like that before, and it was exciting.

The folks along the street were eyeballing us as we bolted past, and a bunch of little kids barely got out of our way. I could hear some mothers screaming at me, but I didn't stop. I had to get to that depot in a hurry, and there was no time to pause and give explanations.

Things were going pretty good until we rounded a corner and hit one of those excuse-me-ma'ams, and that old bump about did us in. First we tipped onto two wheels, and then we crashed back and were on the other two wheels, and I thought for sure we had lost it. Lucky for us that the horse didn't know our predicament, for he kept fogging it along, and our speed eventually brought us back onto all four wheels again. Before anything else could happen, we were churning to a dusty halt near the already moving caboose of the train.

"Let's go, Ida Mae!" I shouted as we leaped from the surrey. Then I shouted back at Sister Dunn. "Much obliged, ma'am. We're all done now. Thanks for your timely assistance."

"Yes, young man," she answered sweetly, as she whipped her horse around, "and I'm all Dunn, too." She started giggling then at her pun, and Ida Mae and I laughed, too.

The conductor on the Sanpete Crawler was Amos Reed Tucker, and he had been conductor for as long as I could recall. Most folks knew him as Amos, although for me he was "Tucker Bill," a name he had told me to call him years before when I was just a little squirt. I'd always thought of him as my good friend, and right then I couldn't have had a better friend for helping me save Pa.

"Well, if it isn't my good buddy Hy," he said as we entered the door of the caboose. "Why, it's been a month of Sundays since I saw you, young feller. And ain't this the Sorenson girl? What on earth are you two up to?"

"Tucker Bill," I replied breathlessly, "we've got more troubles than a cow in a cornpatch. This here's Ida Mae Sorenson, like you said, and together she and I are trying to save Pa before someone hangs up his hide."

"Say, that's right," Tucker Bill said thoughtfully. "Today is your Pa's race, isn't it? I heard tell of it down in Manti, and I hate to say it, but most folks down thataway think your Pa's going to lose. What in the world got into him, Hy?"

"It's not what got into Bishop Soderberg," Ida Mae blurted. "It's what got into my father that has us worried. That's why we have to get to Santaquin, and fast."

"Santaquin! Miss Sorenson, if I owned houses in hell and in Santaquin, I'd live in hell and rent out the one in Santaquin. What could you ever want there?"

"Nothing, exactly," I said, grinning. "It's just that Santaquin is where we have to be if we want to save Pa."

"Now hold up, you two. Let's start at the top and work down on this thing."

So between the two of us we told Tucker Bill about Ida Mae's father, how he wanted to be bishop, and was willing to do anything to destroy Pa so that could happen. We also told him about the problems in Santaquin, and how we had to get there before Pa did, or he was had for sure.

When we had finished, Tucker Bill sat in silence for a moment, and then he spoke. "Well, if that doesn't beat all I've ever heard. And that trick with the woman lying in the dirt and groaning will stop Bishop Soderberg sure as snow in winter. He's got more mercy and compassion for the hurts of others than any man I ever saw."

"Tucker Bill, can we beat Pa to Santaquin?"

"Good question, Hy! Good question! As far as I know, it's never been done. And up to now I'd have said it couldn't be done, either. Thing is, now it about has to be, so we'll just have to change our minds and do it. And by jimbo, we will! Hy, are you afraid of heights? Jiggly, wiggly, shaky, rolling-along-fast kind of heights?"

"Huh?"

"Hyrum, there ain't no way we can do what you need without a full head of steam. We've got to let the engineer, Delbert Yergeson, know of our straits, and then he's got to have help feeding the hopper. Hy, there's no way that I am allowed to leave this caboose, so that leaves just you and Ida Mae. One of you is going to have to climb out and crawl along the top of the five cars between here and the engine."

Well, I gulped and swallowed hard, because I knew for certain who it wasn't going to be. I'd never let Ida Mae up on that swaying walkway.

"Tucker Bill, how do I get up on the roof?"

Ida Mae squeezed my arm and gave me a look that would have melted snowbanks, and right then I would have fought bears in a tunnel at midnight for that girl.

Tucker Bill grinned and opened the door, and before I knew it I was making my way across the roof of the first car, wondering what in blazes I was doing there. We all made fun of that train, calling it the crawler and such, but on top of that car it felt like we were moving at a pretty good clip. And sway? If you've never been on top of a moving railroad car, bumping along on a narrow-gauge track, weaving through the sage and the oak and pines, then you'll never appreciate how I felt. Suffice it to say, I was full of fear and trembling, and would that I might not have been there.

I carefully crawled across that first car, feeling about as wary as a loafer wolf moving upwind into a baited buffalo carcass. There I climbed to my feet and leaped to the second car, and was just falling to my stomach for the next crawl when the train gave a powerful lurch. Instantly I was thrown off the walk, and then I found myself sliding slowly toward the edge of the car. Well, in an instant I was as scared as a bull elk being ringed by a pack of half-starved wolves, and it wasn't just because I was falling off, either, though that was certainly part of it. You see, I knew that if I fell off that train, then it was all over for Pa, and that had me scared. Then, too, Ida Mae was watching, and nobody likes to get killed in front of his girl. So wildly I started grabbing, trying to catch on to something, anything that would slow my fall. But there was nothing, nothing but the smooth wooden top of the car.

Ida Mae was screaming as my feet went over the edge, and I reckon I was praying louder than she was screaming. But I was praying without hope, for I knew I was a goner. There was no way that I was going to stop, and my pounding heart told me I was right. However, it was then that a miracle happened. At the last minute my index finger slipped neatly into a knothole, and instinctively I held on.

Now, I might mention that due to my bad leg I had been forced, over the years, to develop and use my arms and my shoulders, and so I had a lot of strength in them. At that moment I was surely thankful for that strength. By inches I muscled myself back up onto that roof, listening while I did it to Ida Mae, who was crying and cheering me on all at once. I know she thought I was a dead man, and for a time I thought so as well. Finally, though, I was back on the walk, and after a quick wave to reassure Ida Mae, I nervously resumed my ordeal.

The rest of the way I had no troubles, and after about a month of terror I dropped down into the tender right behind Delbert Yergeson.

"Mr. Yergeson, sir," I blurted, assuming that he was aware I had dropped in.

I've seen men jump before, but never as high or as far or as fast as Brother Yergeson did that day. You'd have thought I was a ghost the way he looked at me. He recovered quickly, though, and soon I had recounted the whole story to him. Then he grinned and asked me if I wanted to work for my fare, and to tell you the truth that was the first time I had thought of that little item. I agreed, though, and in no time at all I was stoking the furnace and building up the steam in that mobile boiler unit we called the crawler.

"With enough steam," Brother Yergeson shouted, "we might make it, Hyrum. We just might!"

12

The Herder and the Cinch Strap

As Bishop Jons Soderberg pushed his big bay stud across the Divide, he found his mind dwelling upon his own ineptness, both as a horseman and as a bishop. How, he wondered, could a man live in a country where so much depended upon horses and still know so little about them? Yet that wasn't entirely true, and he knew it. In fact, he knew quite a bit about horses. He just couldn't ride them very well. He was a livestock man, an animal breeder, and he was the first to admit it. That was why he had been so impressed with Ingersol that first day down near Ephraim.

A magnificent animal, obviously a worker, Ingersol had impressed him like no horse ever had. He remembered looking into the huge bay's mouth, examining all forty teeth, the grinders and tusks as well as the front ones, and all were strong and evenly worn. The black cavities of the bottom center nippers were clearly visible, which meant that the horse was not yet six years old. In fact, the bishop was certain he was nearer four.

The animal's head was well sculptured and held high, a sure sign of pride. His ears, small and pointed, were wide apart, as were his eyes, which were full, large, and uncommonly alert. His neck was long and tapering, the muscles thick on top and thinning toward the middle. His back was short, but his hips, close-jointed, were long and broad. His withers were located exactly halfway between his ears and the coupling of the hip, and all this gave the bishop confidence that the horse could sustain a man his size. The clincher, though, was the width of the animal's chest and hips. This horse, the bishop knew immediately, had speed and bottom. Yet the really remarkable thing, notwithstanding these fine points, was the aminal's deceptive gait. When he moved he looked big and awkward. In the saddle, however, one was instantly aware of the animal's smoothness, speed, and grace. He was literally what was called a "rocking-chair" horse.

Eighteen hundred dollars was an awful lot of money—the bishop knew that. There were many reasons why one didn't pay that much for a horse. The first reason, of course, was simple economics. A horse would have to perform long and hard to recoup such an awesome investment.

Another problem was the image such an investment presented. By nature the bishop worried little about the envious or childish thoughts of others. Because he was a bishop, however, there was a problem. Anything he did, no matter what, that appeared foolish or sinful had the potential of becoming a stumbling block in the path of faith which his ward members were following. He wished it weren't so, yet nevertheless it was a truism that far too many people judged the Church by the actions of their bishop. Obviously that meant their testimonies were weak, but still they were sons and daughters of God, and he was duty-bound to live a life that would strengthen rather than hinder their spiritual growth. So that was the second consideration.

The third consideration, however, was the real clincher, and it went opposite to the first two. Besides being bishop, Soderberg was also the most wanted polygamist in Sanpete County, Territory of Utah, and as such he was forever being pursued by federal marshals. As bishop, he felt honor-bound to avoid capture no matter what the cost.

After all, it was the prophet, John Taylor, who had recently said: "Avoid [the marshals] as much as you possibly can—just as you would wolves, or hyenas, or crocodiles, or snakes. . . . Get out of their way as much as you can. What! Won't you submit to the dignity of the law? Well, I would if the law would only be a little more dignified.''

Undoubtedly President Taylor's feelings had been influenced by his experience forty-four years before, when he lay beneath the bed in the Carthage jail, suffering from wounds caused by four lead balls received when his beloved prophet, Joseph Smith, was murdered.

"Yes," Bishop Soderberg said aloud, ''he was justified in preaching rebellion, and so am I! For is not my own baby daughter mouldering in the grave because of the injustice of mobs wearing on their chests the authority of the United States government?''

And so his decision was made. He had paid the eighteen hundred dollars for the Belgian stud, and now he was suffering one of the inevitable consequences. If only he had cautioned Victoria against discussing the price he had paid for his horse! He hadn't, though; the word had quickly spread, and now he was left with only hindsight, a poor substitute for wisdom and discretion.

Always Jons Soderberg had prided himself on being his own man, and rightly so. Now, however, as he raced away from the morning sun, he realized that was no longer true. He had allowed the heavy foot of pride to trample down his well-nurtured free agency. The stinging taunts and shallow laughter of Brother Sorenson and the others should never have affected him.

But they had!

"Jumping blue blazes!'' he murmured softly. ''As a bishop, as a man of God, why didn't I rise above such pettiness? Like Nephi of old, I am moved to declare: 'O wretched man that I am! Yea, my heart sorroweth because of my flesh; my soul grieveth because of mine iniquities.'

"Dear, dear Father," he groaned, ''why don't I ever learn? I promised thee up at the Big Springs, after I was called to be bishop, that I would put away my foolish pride. Why, instead of helping Brother Mungus, I fell into Satan's trap, and have only hedged his celestial progress a little further! Lord, bless Brother Mungus. Help him to—''

Bishop Soderberg winced as his horse lunged over the lip of a deep wash, and suddenly he had to swerve to avoid colliding with none other than Rasmus "Pain" Mumford.

"Whooaahh!" he shouted, sawing back on the reins. "Brother Mumford . . . Pain . . . what are you doing here? And why are you holding that torch?"

Pain Mumford stood flat-footed, his mouth hanging open, feeling the red of guilt and embarrassment flush across his face.

"Why . . . ah . . . Bishop . . . ," he stuttered, struggling desperately to stamp out the blazing fire-brand. "How'd you get here so quick? Ah . . . I mean . . . er . . . what are you doing out so bright and early?"

Soderberg was thoughtfully silent as realization flooded his mind. Slowly then a smile spread over his face, and quietly he spoke again.

"Pain, you'd best be careful with that fire. Grass this time of year burns easily. In fact, seeing that burning patch over there puts me in mind of the time some owl-hoots fired the prairie out in Wyoming just so they could stampede a few head of stock. Wind changed, though, and they came fair to burning down all of Cheyenne before they got it under control. Of course, they were bad men, Pain. Real bad! And real dead, too, when the vigilantes got through with them. Seems that folks don't like their homes burned down. No, sir, they don't like that at all.

"But I was thinking. Wind right here is coming out of the canyon, blowing across the Divide and straight toward Aspen Wells. Be a real shame if we were to lose our town now, wouldn't it? But of course, that's why you're here, isn't it? To put out that fire. I'll say this, my friend, folks'll be mighty proud when I tell them how Brother Pain Mumford saved our town from the ravages of a range fire. Yes, sir, they'll be mighty proud!"

The bishop then reined around and spurred the Belgian forward, calling back as he did.

"One thing more, Pain. You be sure to tell Brother Mungus how slick you put out that fire. He'll be thrilled to know."

Rapidly then he rode off, leaving Pain Mumford standing in the middle of a slowly spreading circle of fire, leaving him wondering just how much the bishop really did know.

"By golly," Pain muttered in amazement as he moved to contain the fire, "Bishop Soderberg is quite a man. He had me dead to rights, and then he gave me an out. From now on when my hand goes up in meeting to sustain that man, I'm going to mean it. Jons Soderberg is my kind of bishop!"

Jons Soderberg, meanwhile, was thundering toward the canyon, his thoughts racing as rapidly as were the hooves of his horse.

"Pain Mumford," he said aloud. "I wonder what Mungus did to get Pain under his thumb. Why, just last week Pain brought his two finest lambs into the tithing office. Had a good chat with him, too. I wonder if his wife's doing any better? I sent my counselors to see her, but maybe I should have gone myself. Blasted horse race! Got so worked up over this race that I forgot just where my priorities were. Pain Mumford is a fine man. Fact is, I wouldn't hesitate recommending Pain to replace me as bishop.

"Dear Heavenly Father, this race is about the most foolish thing I've ever done. But thou knowest how much I've taken from Mungus, and thou also knowest how much I've taken from Marshal Clawson and the other legal authorities our government has set against us. And . . . well, I know all this is nothing compared to the suffering of thy Son, or even the suffering of the prophets. But Lord, I'm no prophet, I'm just Jons Soderberg, and now I'm in trouble clean up to my eyebrows because I went and got weak when I shouldn't have. I know I've no right to ask for help, Heavenly Father, but I'm asking for it just the same. If there is any way, any way at all for me to get out of this mess, why, I'll. . . . "

For a time the bishop rode in silence, deeply concerned about the far-reaching and potentially disastrous consequences of his horse race. Suddenly, though, as he emerged from a clump of cottonwoods, he glanced up, his countenance changed, and he spoke again.

"Glory be, Father," he whispered reverently, "I've never seen this canyon so beautiful. Look at how the sun is splashing so vividly across the peaks of Nebo! And look at those quakies—leaves just dancing in the breeze. And green? I don't remember ever seeing the canyon so fresh, so crisp, so green. Why, even those old cedars set my soul to singing this morning! What is it, Father? What are you trying to tell me?''

His voice trailed off and he rode in silence for a time totally immersed in the ethereal beauty of Salt Creek Canyon. Soderberg could never remember feeling quite this way, and he was totally without words to describe it. It was almost an emotional thing. In fact, it was affecting his emotions to the point that—

Snap!

Soderberg knew instantly that his cinch strap had broken, and it was only by dint of mighty effort that he was able to hold himself and his saddle onto the horse while he reined in. Awkwardly then he slid to the side, his saddle coming with him, and both he and the saddle fell in a heap beneath the stallion's nervous feet. Extricating himself hurriedly, he began examining his gear to discover the nature of his problem, which he knew was serious. It was obvious that the strap had been cut, and it was also obvious that it had been done in such a was that it could not be repaired. Blast! If only he hadn't given his old double-rigged rim-fire saddle to his sons. That had two straps, and he could have managed. But this new-fangled single-rig—or center-fire, as they were calling it—had one strap only; it was cut, and now he was in trouble. Suddenly he thought of his own belt, reached for it, and remembered that he had left it off that day, wearing his suspenders instead. So what was left to do? Well, two choices were all he could see: The first was to continue bareback, the other was to end the race right here. It was obvious that he couldn't do the latter, but he know he'd never last the full distance without a saddle. Perhaps, though, it might be possible to pick one up along the way. Oh, if only he knew who'd cut that strap! If only—

"Say, bishop, that young feller did a nice job, didn't he?"

Bishop Soderberg, startled out of his reverie, spun his head to see an old man seated on a rock beside the trail directly behind him. Amazed, the bishop spun to his feet, wondering how he could have ridden past the old man without having seen him. Under inspection the old man wasn't too impressive. His hair and beard were white, and his clothing, though clean, was obviously well worn. His face was wrinkled like an old apple, but out of that face flashed eyes like none the bishop had ever seen before. They were clear and blue, but at times almost seemed filled with a flashing fire. Of course that was silly, but by golly, that was what the old man's eyes looked like. And for some reason he looked familiar, too, though the bishop was certain he'd never seen him before.

Could this be one of Mungus's men? No, of course he wasn't. As quickly as he thought it, the bishop knew that this man could not be a part of that crowd. But if not that, then who was he, and what was he doing in the canyon? And what did he mean about a young feller doing a nice job?

"Howdy," the bishop said, wondering just what he should say. "What young feller did what?"

For a moment the old man sat silently, carefully regarding the bishop. Then suddenly he smiled and spoke, his voice so quiet that Jons Soderberg found himself straining to hear.

"Why, the young feller who cut your strap. He did a nice job. You can't repair it."

"Young feller? Do you know who did it?"

"Well, no, not exactly, though I could tell you what he looked like and even his name if it was necessary. Only it isn't."

"Say, how do you know who it was, old man? Were you there?"

"Bishop, your questions are difficult ones to answer. I was there in some respects, though you may put your thoughts to rest concerning my involvement. I had nothing to do with it, but only observed the deed from a great distance off. At that point I had not received permission to come, and so was still supposedly an impartial observer. Now, however, you have asked for help, so I have been allowed to work with you."

Soderberg looked at him blankly, understanding nothing of what the old man was saying.

"Say," he asked, "do I know you?"

"I don't imagine you do. Though you might, you might at that. Lots of folks have, one time or another. Maybe you read about me. Time to time I kept a journal. Maybe you read that."

"Are you a sheepherder?" the bishop asked, looking around for sign of a herd. "I don't recall passing any sheep."

"Why, I'd guess you'd say I was a sheepherder, all right. At least that business is the only one I've worked at for quite a spell. But you're right. I've not much of a herd around here. It's what you'd call a family flock, but I think you'd have to say it's sort of scattered."

"Why, man," the bishop replied angrily, "that's no way to treat livestock! A herder is the leader of the sheep; he gives a herd guidance and direction. He protects them from danger, takes care of injuries, and so on. How can you do that if you aren't with your herd? It's no wonder they're scattered. How long has it been since you worked with them?"

"Oh, not long. In fact, I work with one or another of them most every day."

"Say, who do you herd for?"

"Oh, nobody local. Why?"

"Well," stormed the bishop, "if you herded for me, I'd want to know that you had left my herd! That's why!"

"Then what would you do?"

"Why, by golly, I'd find out why you left my herd. And if the reason wasn't good enough, I'd fire you! That's what I'd do!"

"Bishop, I like that. I like a man who'll say what he thinks even if the other feller might not like it. And I like a man who cares about his livestock, who cares enough to buy the very best. Like that Belgian stallion there, for instance."

"Well," Soderberg replied, somewhat embarrassed, "I've always said that a man ought to buy the best and only cry once."

"Interesting idea. Very interesting."

"So you like my horse, huh?"

"I certainly do. It is a marvelous animal."

"Well, that makes a grand total of two of us who like him. Not exactly a majority, I'd say."

"No, it isn't. Not normally. Bishop, I understand that you are in a fix. So I am here to help you out."

"So the word has spread out of Sanpete County, has it? Well, old-timer, whoever told you I was in a fix had it pegged about right. For I surely am in trouble. But it isn't the kind of a fix that I can get helped out of."

"Why not?" the old man asked.

"Because it's a fix I fixed for myself, is why. I danced the tune, and now I have to pay the fiddler."

"Now, that is interesting. I was told that your fix had to do with a horse race, not a dance. Maybe I was misinformed."

Jons Soderberg gave the old man a narrow look, wondering if he was funning him. But the old fellow surely did seem serious. Maybe he was, but had just been out at the herd too long. Yes, that had to be it. He'd probably been alone so long that he had slipped a cog. The bishop had seen it happen before, plenty of times, so this poor fellow wouldn't be the first. Suddenly he realized that time was passing, and that he had to be on his way.

"Mister," he said, "I've got to go. I've got me a race to win."

"Hold up, bishop. I'm not through with you. You just said your trouble was a dance, and now you say it is a race. Just what is your problem?"

He was so serious that Soderberg burst out laughing, and in spite of his hurry he turned back and quickly told the old man about his fix.

"So that's it," he said. "Naturally, I'd like to win the race. I think old Ingersol here can do it, and given half a chance, we will. Or we would have, if this cinch-strap hadn't been cut. The real problem, though, isn't the race. It's my ward. I'm just sick about what I'm doing to them."

"What do you mean?"

"Well, a man who becomes bishop has got to be above the little problems that seem to afflict mankind—problems such as pride, arrogance, selfishness, dishonesty, and so on. A bishop sort of makes a covenant with the Lord that he will be the spiritual beacon for all the people in his ward. By letting social pressure push my pride into gear, I've in essence told my whole ward that gambling is A-OK with me.

I've also told them, pretty clearly, that Mungus Sorenson is my enemy. Can you imagine that? Why, Mungus is a good man, and I'll tell you, I'm amazed at his leadership ability. Somehow I've got to find a way to reach him. Somehow I have to let him know that we need him, and that we need the rest of the men who hang out with him. Sure, they have a few problems, but so do I, and so does everyone else in the ward. None of us are perfect, and I have come to the conclusion that the Lord doesn't expect any of us to be; all he demands is that we be moving in the right direction. And that is what I'd like to help Mungus understand. If I could work that out, either by winning or losing this race, then I'd do it!''

"Bishop, are you certain that winning isn't as important as helping Brother Sorenson? In your heart of hearts can you declare that to be true?''

"Yes, I can! Last night I couldn't have, nor would I have said so this morning. But now I feel different about it. Trouble is, old man, that I don't know which would help those men the most—winning or losing.''

"Winning would, bishop. And because you have conquered your pride and set your heart back in the right place, I'm willing to help you do it. You have learned that a mistake is only a mistake if one persists in it. If one's course is changed, then a mistake becomes a learning experience. You've learned, so I'll help.''

"Oh, brother!'' Jons Soderberg thought. "That's all I need, a little help from this slightly cracked old egg. Why, if—''

"Listen carefully, young man, for here is what you must do:

> "Canter from one
> gallop from two
> ride light in the saddle
> and run from
> three.
>
> "To Brother Sorenson
> be kind *and* firm
> and of a truth
> he will come to
> thee.''

Smiling then, the old man lifted his hand.

"Farewell, good bishop. Race well. The animal you have there is worthy of a good run."

Well, to say that the bishop was confused would have been to say it mildly.

"Say," he stammered. "What . . . why . . . how do you . . . who . . . ?"

"Yes, bishop? If you have something to say, say it. I've got things to do that are a whole lot more important than sitting here on a rock listening to you stutter. And, by the way, so do you. So say what you have a mind to say, and then be on your way."

Open-mouthed in amazement, the bishop stared at the old man. For the life of him he didn't know what to make of the old fellow. He'd certainly never met anyone like him.

"Fine," he said finally. "One question. Who are you?"

"Bishop, I've already told you that names aren't very important. I can't tell you mine. I won't even tell you that we're related, for you wouldn't believe that. But I will tell you something that is important, if you'd like."

"I certainly would."

"Very well. You have a broken cinch-strap. What do you propose to do about it?"

"Well, I don't know, exactly. I—"

"Merciful heavens!" the old man exclaimed. "Bishop, don't you carry a spare cinch-strap in your saddlebags?"

"A spare cinch-strap? Old man, I think your own cinch is getting a little frayed. Why would I ever carry a spare cinch-strap with me?"

"Bishop, that is a foolish question. You'd carry a spare cinch-strap around just in case one of your fellowmen was low-down enough to cut the one you were using. Like that young man obviously was. But you didn't answer me. Do you have a spare?"

"Of course I don't have a spare!"

"Are you certain?"

"Say, I ought to know, hadn't I?"

"Yes, you certainly ought to know. Nevertheless, were I you I'd check in my saddlebags. In fact, let's see . . . yes, I'd check in your right saddlebag if I were you."

"Why? All that bag has in it is my lunch. I know. I packed it myself."

The old man then grinned. "Mighty funny taste you have, bishop. Very few men would eat leather for lunch. Take a look, bishop."

"Oh, for crying out loud! I. . . ."

And the bishop, to his total amazement, opened his right saddlebag to find, neatly coiled on top of his lunch, a new cinch-strap.

"Well, don't just stand there staring, bishop. Get it changed! You've got a race to run."

Without another word the bishop changed straps. Quickly then he saddled up and remounted, forced a grin at the calm old man, waved weakly, and slapped his spurs to his horse.

"Humph," he said as he galloped off. "I wonder how that old man knew about the new strap? In fact, I wonder which of my wives had the foresight to slip that spare one in? Fact is, I wonder when she did it? But that old man is surely something. I wonder who he works for? Poor old fellow has obviously spent too much time alone at the herd. I do wish he'd told me his name, though. Maybe I could help him. Related, hah! Man must be crazy, thinking I'd believe that. Still, he did look familiar, somehow."

Onward then he galloped, onward through the rocks and grass and trees of the Salt Creek Canyon morning. And as he rode he thought of the old man, and of Mungus and the rest of his ward. What a privilege it was to be called as their bishop! Yes, it took a lot of his time, and yes, he was always giving more than he felt he had to give, but he had been blessed with far more than he had ever given. So far, he had never been able to get the Lord in his debt.

In the midst of his reverie, Soderberg's thoughts were shattered by the crashing explosion of gunfire. Twisting in the saddle the bishop looked back to see three riders come boiling out of the draw he had just ridden past.

"What in tarnation!" he growled, as he heard the *whap* of a bullet passing somewhere near him. "Why, those gents are firing at me!"

Slapping his spurs to his horse's flanks, Bishop Soderberg urged the animal to even greater speed. For a moment he worried about the horse's ability to respond, but then he glanced back and realized two things. The first, and perhaps least significant, was that he was definitely drawing ahead of his pursuers, and rapidly, too. His second realization was that, even though the three men had bandanas over their faces, he recognized one and perhaps two of the horses they were riding.

That lineback dun with the white splash on its chest just had to be Ollie Johnson's, and the dapple gray looked an awful lot like the cayuse Jesse Christensen rode. Setting his jaw, the bishop grimly acknowledged that Mungus certainly had a great deal of power over these men. The third rider would have to be either Loose-lip Lundstrom or Anson Holman, and he would guess from the way the man sat in his saddle that it would be Anson. How in the world could Anson, being the kind of a man he was, justify this?

For five full minutes the four men rode furiously through the narrows of the canyon. Thundering through Hop Creek they rode across the flats where Heber Ockey was clearing off a ranch. Bishop Soderberg kept to the main trail, splashing across Salt Creek and then skirting the southern tip of the Petticoat Cliffs. He knew he was pulling away from the three men, yet he also knew that Ingersol could not endure the terrific pace too much longer. At least he couldn't if the bishop intended that the horse last the remaining ninety-nine miles.

Suddenly from behind him came another flurry of gunfire, and he twisted again to see the two white mares of Mungus Sorenson come crashing down out of the timber, their riders in reckless pursuit of the erstwhile outlaws. For a moment there was concentrated gunfire, and then the three men from Aspen Wells scattered, heading their mounts into the hills in three different directions.

"Oh, no!" the bishop groaned as he glanced back, "now what's going on? Those mares belong to Mungus, I know that! What is he doing fighting his own men?"

As he watched, the two white mares came together and their riders held a hasty conference. Suddenly they broke apart and wheeled

111

in his direction, intent upon renewing the chase the others had so recently abandoned.

In despair the bishop glanced down at his horse. Ingersol was heavily lathered, and foam was flying from his jaws. Still, he was running well, and Soderberg could detect no weakness in him, no weakness at all. But how much longer could he go like this? How much longer could he keep up his killing pace? If it was Mungus and one of his cronies back on those mares, then they were most certainly after him. Yet if it were Mungus, why had he driven off the other three men? That made no sense, not unless Mungus was trying to protect him. But no, that couldn't be it, either. Mungus would be the last person to protect him from injury or danger. So what was going on?

Suddenly he thought of the old man, the old sheepherder who had stopped him earlier. What was it the old fellow had said? Something about a canter, a gallop, and a run? At the time the old man seemed to be rambling, and the bishop had paid little attention to him. But now he wondered. Could the old man have known? Might that old man in some way have seen these men, learned of their plans, and hurried to meet the bishop? Might it be a trap that Mungus was setting, and the old man had learned of it? It was possible, he supposed, though he couldn't imagine how the old fellow might have done it.

"Canter from one," he'd said. That was it! "Canter from one, gallop from two, ride light in the saddle and run from three." Well, if that was a warning, then he'd better heed it. Trouble was, what did the old man mean? He had been running from three, now there were just two, and that ought to mean that he could slow to a gallop. But then maybe the old fellow had meant that he could canter from the first problem, gallop from the second, and that he'd better run like blue blazes from the third. If that was what the old man had meant, then he'd better—

The piercing shriek of the whistle of the Sanpete Valley train ripped apart the still air of the canyon; once, then twice, a long and drawn-out whistle that Soderberg thought would have raised the dead. The stallion leaped forward at the sound, and the bishop, who had anticipated no such movement, was almost unseated. Retaining his seat, however, he glanced back to find, to his amazement, that one of the white mares was riderless and was buckjumping back up the canyon. The other was running wildly toward the hills to the north despite her rider's obvious displeasure, and Soderberg immediately realized that he knew exactly what the old man had meant. From these two he could now slow to an easy lope or gallop, rest his mount, and still maintain his lead. It was simple. Only how could that old man have known that the train would come along and whistle when it did? There was no way that he could have known that. Not unless—but no, that was impossible. Still. . . .

Ahead now he could see the gypsum quarry, and beyond that was the valley where nestled the city of Nephi. Pulling his watch out, he studied it. He had left Aspen Wells at just a little past six in the morning; it was now nearly seven-thirty, and he had almost beaten the sunrise. If it hadn't been for that cut cinch-strap and that crazy old man—

Without warning the Belgian stud leaped sideward, and Jons Soderberg found himself clinging with one hand and one leg to the saddle while the rest of him flopped awkwardly in the air. Briefly he caught a glimpse of a rattlesnake his horse had shied from, and then all he saw was ground and sky and horse and ground and sky again, rapidly and not necessarily in that order. Desperately he pulled himself toward the saddle, using all the strength of his arms to hang on while his horse lunged up the steep hill. After a moment they topped out on the rim, and not until then did the bishop regain his seat. While he caught his breath the horse continued to flee forward, and they covered several hundred yards before the bishop thought to rein the animal in.

"Whew," he sighed as the horse blew and snorted beneath him. "That was a close one. Blasted snake . . . I could have lost the entire race right then."

And that was when he noticed, directly below him in the mouth of the canyon, a herd of milling cattle. It was a big herd of shorthorns, tightly bunched, and Soderberg could tell immediately that anyone trying to get past them on the trail would have problems, at least for a few minutes.

113

"Say," he thought aloud. "I wonder if . . .? Uh-huh. Just as I thought. That herd of cattle right there can't be an accident! Now where is the drover? . . . Ah, yes. Now if he'll . . . that's it, now this way a little more, out from behind those trees, and. . . . Well, I'll be doggoned. That's Osrow "Scar" Thomas down there! I didn't know he was in with Mungus, too. Glory be! Won't surprises ever cease?"

"Hey, Scar!" he shouted. "Scar, I'm up here! *Hello!* I was just passing by, and I thought I'd best say hello. Wish we had time to chat, but I've got to get to Salt Lake City. Come into my office next Sunday, though. I'd like to have a visit with you!"

Soderberg watched with interest and amusement as the expression on Scar's face changed from one of curiosity to understanding and recognition.

"Soderberg!" he shouted, sounding surprised and sick all at the same time. "I thought you'd been held up back there . . . er . . . I mean, I thought you'd been detained."

"Not hardly."

"But how did you get up there?"

"Scar, I like to travel the high places, not the low ones. I try to keep my eyes up, not down. My father used to tell me, Scar, that it is better to aim at the sun and miss than to aim at a pile of manure and hit it. Scar, from the smell down there, I think you've been aiming a little low."

For a moment the bishop thought Scar was going to charge his horse at the sheer hillside. But then he stopped, looked back up the canyon toward Aspen Wells like he was trying to make up his mind, and then he whirled and rode off, kicking his mount like the devil himself was on his trail.

Back up the canyon the train came in sight once more, whistled, and the bishop waved back at whoever it was in the cab who was waving at him. Wheeling his horse then, he turned north across the hills toward Provo and Salt Lake City, while behind him in the canyon Scar flogged his horse toward Aspen Wells, and the outlaw known as Blue John swore bitterly as he trudged along in the dust of Silvertip's white mare, doing his best to catch up with his companion and his runaway mare.

114

13

The Trouble with Being Crippled

There are times a man gets so excited about something that he becomes absolutely certain that it will work out. And there are folks who will tell you that if a man wants something badly enough, he'll get it, no matter what. Mostly I suppose that is true, but nothing except death is ever sure-fire. So when I give advice now I always say to think positive but plan negative. That way, if something doesn't work out just right, you won't kill yourself with disappointment and frustration. You'll just keep on trying for the next time. That was one of the lessons I learned that day while chasing Pa with the train.

The other thing I learned, or rather re-learned, was that just because a fellow prays about something, even prays with all his heart, doesn't mean that the Lord will necessarily let it happen that way. As an example, all my life I'd been praying about my bad foot, praying either that God would make it better or that he'd make people stop laughing at me and poking fun at me. Well, Pa heard me one night, praying for God to smite Pete Livingston because he'd beat the tar out of me. After I'd climbed into bed, Pa came in and sat down beside me. He tickled me a mite and then told me what he thought about my prayer.

He wasn't mad or anything, though. He just told me he'd heard me and thought, after dealing with Heavenly Father himself for lots of years, that I was praying for something that God might not want to give me. I asked why, and he told me that mostly God didn't like to take away the agency of folks, their freedom to act like they wanted. That had been the devil's idea in the first place, and God had rejected it right off. Then Pa told me that people have the freedom to act like they want to act—they just don't have the freedom to choose the consequences of those acts. Consequences were predetermined in heaven, and that's where blessings and punishments come in. If we do something good, then we get a blessing or so for doing it. If we do something bad, then we lose a blessing and so suffer a punishment. Those are the rules that we all agreed to before we were ever born. God lives by them, and so do we—not because we always want to, but because that's the way it is.

What Pa said made sense, and after I'd thought about it for a minute it came to me just how dumb it was to be going around being wicked, fighting and quarreling, stealing eggs and melons, telling lies, and all that other nonsense. My only reward for that was grief and lots of lost blessings, and to tell you the truth, I can't afford to lose any blessings. I'm the kind of fellow who needs all he can get.

So I asked Pa what he thought I ought to be praying for, and he told me Ma and him had been praying about my bad foot right along, and it had come to them that the Lord had given me that foot as a blessing. Well, that made me grin, for I've been dragging that foot around since who flung the chunk, and since when has it been a blessing? I said as much, so Pa told me about Enoch and Moses, who both had speech problems. Yet God called both of them to be prophets. That didn't make much sense to me, so I asked Pa why God had made those men defective, especially if he knew they were going to have to go around preaching the Gospel.

"Hyrum, pretty near anybody can preach. But hardly anybody can be a prophet. That takes somebody who is especially humble and prayerful. If you were a prophet, and all you could do was stutter and stammer, would that make you humble or proud?''

"Humble."

"It's obvious then, isn't it? When God gave Enoch and Moses speech problems, he was in reality giving them special blessings. That was humility, for if those brethren were humble, then the Lord could work with them and make them even greater than they were. If a man has to rely on God, then that same man gets closer to God."

"OK, I guess that makes sense. So what is my great blessing?"

Pa laughed and tousled my hair around a bit, and then he took hold of my shoulders and got real serious.

"Hyrum, how fast can you run?"

"Be funny," I replied bitterly.

"Can you keep up with your brothers?"

"Not hardly."

"There's your blessing. Your Ma and I have noticed that you can hardly wait for anything. When you want something it has to be right now or you get pretty wild. Are we right?"

"Yeah, I reckon."

"Son, that's called not having any patience. Your bad foot forces you to slow down, doesn't it? And being slow automatically teaches a man to have patience."

"But Pa, why is patience such a big deal? What's wrong with being in a hurry?"

"Maybe nothing. Thing is, I have noticed that when a man doesn't have patience he generally doesn't have much tolerance or kindness in him, either. If people aren't as fast with something as he thinks they ought to be, then *bam!* he's had it with them. He has no kindness, no understanding, nothing. Now you know that tolerance and kindness are qualities that Jesus wants us to have. The entire message of the gospel is one of love, of caring. With you, I'd say that the Lord wants you to learn those qualities pretty badly. That's one of the reasons at least why he blessed you with your club foot."

Pa kissed me goodnight then and left, and I thought about what he'd said. And funny thing was, the more I thought about it, the more right Pa sounded. By the time I finally went to sleep I was even thinking about thanking Heavenly Father for my special blessing: my bad foot.

Anyway, there I was on that train, shoveling coal and praying with all my heart that we could catch Pa right quick, when Mr. Yergeson shouted and pointed Pa out to me. And that was when I forgot that God doesn't always answer our prayers right off the way we want him to.

I started pulling on the whistle chain, shouting and waving with all my heart, and then I noticed those two white mares that belonged to Mungus. Right away they started to pitch and buck, and then one man was down and both horses were heading for the trees totally out of control. That was when it dawned on me that Pa was being chased. For a moment or two I watched him, but he was paying no attention to us at all. Suddenly his horse, old Ingersol, jumped sideways and headed up the side of a ridge, and I thought Pa had lost it for sure. We turned a bend then, and I lost sight of Pa for a couple of minutes. When I saw him again he was topped out on the ridge, sitting there watching us. I jerked the whistle again and started waving, but Pa only waved back, sat there for a moment, and then turned and disappeared over the ridge.

When he vanished my heart sank clear down to my boots. I had been so certain that we had caught him, and now I was so disappointed that I was ready to quit.

"Gosh, Mr. Yergeson, I thought we'd caught him there, I surely did. I know he saw me, because I saw him wave. Why do you suppose he didn't stop?"

"Why, boy, that's near a half mile over to that ridge, maybe even a little more. And as I recollect, the last time I saw your Pa he had on his nose a pair of spectacles. From that I'd guess that his eyes are going bad. I think he saw the train, he likely saw someone waving, and he waved back just to be friendly. I'd bet two bits against a hoot-owl's hoot that he had no idea it was you waving at him. Why, he'd never suspect you to be on this train."

"No, I suppose he wouldn't," I agreed. "Only now what am I going to do? Pa's already headed for Santaquin."

"Say, young feller, don't be so discouraged. Did you see how

118

your Pa daylighted those whites when you blew that whistle? Why, already you've done him a heap of good. If I'd been alone I'd have never thought of blowing the whistle. So rattle your hocks, boy, and throw more coal. We've got to get you to Santaquin.''

"But you don't go to Santaquin!" I shouted, struggling with another shovelful of coal.

"True enough. But if we hurry we can get to Nephi before the Utah Central pulls out. Then I can talk with old Cale Steiner, the engineer. He's just crusty enough that if he takes it into his head to get you to Santaquin in a hurry, he'll bend the rules to do it.''

"Will he really?''

"Sure he will. You ever seen him?''

"No.''

"Well, he's a little man. Fact is, he told me hisself that he's so short he has to borrow a stepladder to kick a grasshopper on the shin-bone. What I'm saying, Hy, is that after spending his life on the raw end of one joke after another, he just naturally fights for the underdog. Right now, that is you—you and your father. So hustle, boy, and we'll get you there yet.''

So hustle I did, shoveling that coal out of the tender and into the firebox faster than Johnnie-be-quick. And we did build up a good head of steam, too. I'll tell you, we were really rattling down that track, black smoke billowing up behind us for a mile. It was a beautiful sight to see.

But then, as we came around a curve just above the gypsum mine, I saw Mr. Yergeson look ahead and gasp.

"Look out, Hy!'' he shouted. "We've got us a real problem!''

I looked out the window myself then, and what I saw scared the living bejeebies out of me. There, directly ahead of us, was a herd of cattle blocking off the track.

"It's cows!'' I shrieked.

"I'll say it's cows! It's that prize herd of new shorthorns that Swede Jensen just had shipped in. How in thunder did they get loose, and what are they doing here in the canyon?''

Well, I surely didn't know, but then I doubt that Mr. Yergeson was asking me, anyway. Fact is, he was still talking, or maybe he was even praying, I don't know. I do know that I sure was.

''Hy,'' he shouted suddenly, ''hang on! There isn't time to stop, so I'm opening her wide open. Now we'll see if that cowcatcher up front is good for anything or not.''

Suddenly the whistle started screaming again, blast after blast after blast, and we were getting close enough to the cattle that I could see their faces when they turned to see what was making all the racket.

I've noticed before, when I've been herding Pa's cattle, that with the exception of Hepsi, cows are so dumb they don't know enough to come in out of the rain, and they're about as fast-acting as wet gunpowder. So I didn't have much hope that our whistle would do the job. Except I guess there were a few smart cattle in that bunch. Maybe it was because they were shorthorns or something. I don't know. But right off a few of them started scrambling up the sides of that cut, doing their level best to get out of our way.

The whistle screamed again, several times, and more of those critters got the message. Why, a body never saw such scrambling and climbing. For being so crowded it was wonderful how many of them managed to get out of the way before we got there. Out of that whole herd we hit only three . . . well, four if you count that one foolish cow who kicked at us and got flipped end-over-teakettle for her troubles. I watched her, though, and after a few seconds she got up and took off, so she wasn't hurt too badly. Still, I'll bet it will be a spell before she tries kicking a train again. I kind of wished that it had been Hepsi.

One thing, though. That cow-catcher didn't work too well. Fact is, it didn't catch a single cow. About all it did was to divide them asunder, parting them to the right and to the left as we passed by. Was it me, I'd have called it a cow-cleaver or something like that. Would have made a lot more sense.

Shortly thereafter, and without further incident, we emerged from the canyon and clattered up to the depot in Nephi. We had barely stopped when Mr. Yergeson grabbed my arm and ran with me to the already moving Utah Central. Quickly Mr. Yergeson introduced me to Mr. Steiner and told him my story, and by the time he'd finished, Mr. Steiner was grinning from ear to ear. Jerking his thumb toward the back he motioned for me to get aboard, and then he pulled open the throttle and we were off.

I jumped aboard and was making my way back through the car when I glanced out the window and about had a heart attack. For there, hauling tail along the tracks outside, were an out-of-breath Tucker Bill and a very frightened Ida Mae Sorenson.

"Oh, my goodness," I groaned, "I plumb forgot about Ida Mae!"

I lunged through the car to the back of the platform, reached out, grabbed her arm and pulled. And while Tucker Bill pushed I was glad once again for the strength of my arms. Ida Mae stumbled and was bouncing along like a barrel rolling downhill, but I held on and after a minute she was there beside me on the platform, shaking like quakies in a high wind. Well, I was shaking, too, but I didn't want her to know that, so I tried to make a funny.

"I don't know about you, Ida Mae, but I'm getting awfully tired of just about missing trains."

She grinned and snuggled up to me, I put my arm around her to steady her (I needed a little steadying myself about then), and together we walked into the caboose and sat down. And for the first time in a long time I found myself feeling self-conscious about my drag-along foot. Why? Well, have you ever thought about what it would be like to be walking beside a girl with your arm around her kind of tight? And instead of moving smoothly all you can do is lurch along, either bumping into her or pulling away from her with every step you take? And that when the thing you want most in all the world is to impress her favorably? Think about it for a minute, and you'll understand why it bothered me so much. Right then I felt as out of place as a .22 cartridge in a twelve-gauge shotgun, and I started wondering just what I was trying to prove, pretending I was normal in the presence of such a special girl as Ida Mae.

Right away my ears and neck started to burn, and I was just coming down with a real bad case of feel-sorry-for-me-itis when Ida Mae looked up at me and spoke.

"Hyrum, when you almost fell off the train back there in the canyon, I thought I was going to die. I've never been so scared in my whole life! And pray? I've never cried and prayed so hard, either. Not ever!''

Well, shock me! What she'd said so surprised me that I didn't know what to say. So I just sat there like a dummy and asked how come.

She looked up at me again, her eyes big and round, and I could see that they were watering up right rapidly. Now what was I going to do? Why had I said that? Why . . . ?

"Don't you know, Hyrum? Can't you tell how I feel about you? In my whole life I've never known anyone who was so kind and gentle, who really cared about other people. Why, you're special, Hyrum, and I like you. I like you very much.''

Now my ears were really burning. I couldn't believe what I was hearing. I couldn't believe—

"I was so worried when you started across the top of the train, Hyrum. I mean, with your foot and all I was sure that you were going to—"

Ida Mae suddenly stopped, realizing, I suppose, what she had said. And me, I just dropped my arm from her shoulders and sat there, staring at my twisted foot and wishing I had never been born.

For a long time neither of us spoke, and I didn't look at her to see what she was doing, either. I just sat there trying to think of something to say that would show her how badly she had hurt me. For she had, though for the life of me I couldn't understand why I was so devastated. After all, she had only spoken the truth, and I'd heard it often enough before. I'll tell you, self-pity had come back real quick.

"Yeah," I said finally, making my voice as bitter as I could, working myself into a real mad. "It sure is tough, having to worry about a cripple. And I'll bet it is just as tough being seen with one, isn't it? I must be about as wanted as a polecat at a picnic!''

That started her to crying in earnest, but I didn't look at her. No, sir, I didn't! If I was going to hurt, so was she!

"Hyrum," she sobbed quietly, "I didn't mean—"

"Oh, yes, you did, and you know it, too! I know what my foot looks like. And I know what it looks like when I hobble along, too!

I'll bet that for a sweet little girl like you it must be a real mortifying experience, being seen out in public with a crippled freak like me. Why do you do it? So people will laugh all the harder when they see how much worse I look when I am with you?''

"Hyrum, I—''

"Oh come off it, Ida Mae!'' I stormed, angry now through and through, and wondering that I could have made myself so angry so quickly. "You don't really like me, and you know it! No girl can really like a cripple!''

Suddenly Ida Mae jumped to her feet and slapped me in the face, hard! She was still crying, but now she was mad, more angry than I had ever seen anybody except maybe Pa that time after the marshals abused Aunt Polly and wrecked our house.

"You're right!'' she said, almost spitting her words at me. "I don't like you! But being a cripple has nothing to do with it. Or maybe it does. I liked you because I thought you were sweet and kind, because I thought you were a man who had the kind of qualities that I wanted someday in my husband. But no, you're not like that! I'm not even sure that I would call you a man. You're just a mean and vicious boy, just like my brother Curly and his friend Pete. Of course I noticed your club foot. I'm not blind. Everybody notices things like that! Big deal. I've got freckles, and people notice them, too. So what? I don't like freckles, but I hope that people can look past them, just like I looked past your foot, to see what kind of a person is there. And you know, Hyrum, I liked what I saw so much that I decided that you weren't really crippled at all. It was me who was crippled, because I noticed your foot and let it bother me. So I made up my mind that I wouldn't let it bother me any more. I even prayed about it. And you probably won't believe this, but I haven't thought of it since. At least I hadn't until I saw you start out across the roof of that train. And then I only noticed it because I was so worried about you, because I cared so much about you.

"What do you want? Do you want people to close their eyes when you walk past? Do you want people to pretend and to be dishonest around you? Do you want them to lie and say they don't notice your foot when they really do? Hyrum, you can't help it. It isn't your fault that you were born with a club foot. But neither is it theirs, nor mine! No matter what you or anyone else says, you are different, at least to that extent. And because you are, people will notice it. The thing is, instead of hiding behind it the way you are doing, you ought to be proud that you are you, that you have had experiences and feelings that most of the rest of us will never have. But no, not you! Not Hyrum Soderberg! You're too busy feeling sorry for yourself to even notice how much you have to give.

"Let me tell you something! You're crippled, all right. But it isn't your foot. No, sir, Hyrum Soderberg! You're crippled in your mind, and that is the worst kind of cripple that a man can be!"

And with that she turned and marched through the train and into the next car, slamming the door behind her and leaving me alone to choke down my tears of humiliation and ponder what she had said. And I'll tell you, facing up to that was one of the toughest things I've ever had to do. That was because she was right—she was right, and I knew it. And what made me most angry was that I had gone over all that before, myself, and thought I had it licked. I mean, how long had it been since I'd let it bother me when someone stared at my foot? I didn't know, but it had been a spell, that was certain.

Slowly I got up and hobbled back to the platform behind the caboose. What was wrong with me? Why had I acted like that? Why in the world . . . ?

For a long time I just leaned against the rail, watching the country slipping away behind me. The land north of Nephi was pretty arid, growing mostly rocks and dirt. And the brush on the lower slopes of Mt. Nebo was so thick that the rabbits had to climb trees just to look out. Here and there some hardy farmer had practically drowned himself in his own sweat clearing the land of brush and rocks, and was now trying to grow dry-land grain, though most farmers were lucky if they got more than ten to twelve bushels to the acre. Still, they were doing their best to put the land to use, to make it productive—and knowing that made me feel proud.

You see, they were Mormons, I was a Mormon, and that sort of put us all on the same team. Being productive was a part of our religion. So was doing the best we could with what we had and not complaining about what we didn't have. Joseph Smith taught that, Brigham Young taught it, and now Wilford Woodruff, who was Acting President of the Church since the death of John Taylor, was teaching it. You see, we believe that the land is the Lord's (though why he wants some of it I'll never know) and when a man is allowed to use it, even if he buys it first, he is still obligated to the Lord to do the most with it that he possibly can. I think Pa calls that the law of stewardship.

And the law of stewardship doesn't cover just land, either. It deals with everything that we as humans have to deal with. I heard Pa give a discourse on the law of stewardship once, and he explained that the Lord had provided everything for us that we needed in order to be happy, prosperous, and righteous. The Lord made us stewards over everything that affects our lives, and we are under obligation to do the best we can with what the Lord has given us to do it with.

And there was the problem. You see, the Lord had given me my bad foot and had made me steward over it, so to speak. All I had to do was do my best with what I had. And I had been doing my best—or at least it seemed to me that I had. Sure, it wasn't always easy, and sure, I became bitter now and then. But mostly I was handling it. Or at least I was until Ida Mae went and said what she did. Blast! Why does a fellow have to be so gosh-awful dumb? Sometimes I wondered how I ever got past the fly-leaf of my first grade primer. Ma would tell me that my pride was getting in the way of my happiness, and it was. I could even see it. But how is a man supposed to get rid of pride? More and more I was coming to sympathize with Pa.

Shucks! Things would surely be a whole lot more simple if I was dead. For a moment or two I wondered what being dead would be like. I didn't really think about the being dead part, just about what Ida Mae would think if they stopped the train and she came back to apologize and I was gone. They would start a search and would find me lying along the tracks, all battered and broken and bloody, and then wouldn't she be sorry! I could just imagine her crying, saying over and over to herself that it was all her fault, that she really loved me and that she hadn't meant to do it, to say what she'd said. Oh, how sweet is revenge!

I looked down then at the tracks and the ties, speeding away from beneath me. Would it hurt much, I wondered! Probably so, at least for a minute or two. But if I hit right, and didn't try to protect myself. . . .

Oh, good grief, I thought! Hyrum Soderberg, how dumb can you get? That's called suicide, killing yourself! And you know what that means. Murder! Beside, if you died, of course Ida Mae would cry. She'd probably even cry a lot. But sometime she would stop, sometime she wouldn't have any more tears for that fellow, poor old Hyrum what's-his-name, who felt so sorry for himself that he jumped off the train. And after she finally stopped crying, then what? Why, you'd still be dead, Hyrum, old boy. That's what. Crying and feeling bad is only for a little while. Dead is for a long, long time.

Yeah, and besides that, it would be just my luck to not get killed at all. I'd probably just get broken up a lot and become a worse cripple than I already was. Then I'd probably have to drag around two bad feet instead of just one. That would likely be how Heavenly Father would punish me for blowing my stewardship over my body. Isn't life tough? As near as I can tell, nothing is ever easy!

Again I looked at the rails and the ties, speeding away from beneath me, slipping away so fast they were just a blur. But then, when they got far enough away, or I did, they could be seen distinctly. Funny, I thought, how much life is like that. Things around a person happen so fast that everything is a blur. It's hard to tell, until something is past or until you've moved away from it, just exactly what is going on. Like my fight with Pete Livingston, which led to my prayer, which led to Pa telling me about my special blessing. You see, it would have been easy for me to say that the fight was a bad thing, because I lost and about got my nose pushed through the back of my skull. But later that fight turned into a blessing because of what it led to. Makes sense, doesn't it? From a distance, things always look more clear.

Or maybe like my fight with Ida Mae. Now that I thought about it, that little girl meant more to me than anyone else in the whole world, except of course my family. Yet there she was, crying somewhere like her heart was broken because I, the fellow who supposedly liked her, had been meaner than a hydrophoby skunk. Now how much sense did that make?

"Hyrum," I said to myself, "you've got to go apologize to that girl! You've got it to do even if she's as cold as the stare of a gila monster!"

But then, just as I turned to go find her, I saw dust off to the east, up along the foothills. My first thought was of Pa, but after a moment I could tell that it wasn't Pa at all. It was those two white mares again. I couldn't believe it. Already they had come this far, and they were still smoking along like Old Nick was after them. Well, in a way that was good, for it meant that Pa was still ahead of them. Now, if only we could—

"Say, young feller. I've been looking for you."

I turned to see who was speaking, and found the conductor walking toward me through the caboose, shaking his head like he thought I was the most impossible person he'd ever seen.

"Cale Steiner told me that we're trying to get you to Santaquin in a hurry. I told him he shouldn't, that it wasn't good for a train to race it like this. But he just laughed and told me it was important. Ha! You don't look so important. Who are you, anyhow?"

"I—uh—"

"Just as I thought. You ain't nobody. Well, no matter. The damage has been done, and now old Steiner will have to pay for it. It's about time, too. Anyway, that's Santaquin just beyond the next ridge. We'll be pulling in in about five minutes, so find that little lady friend of yours and be ready."

With that he turned and walked off, and I heard him muttering about kids, and about how a cute girl like her must have real problems to be willing to be seen with a freak and a cripple.

Because I couldn't do anything else, I grinned, thinking that his high-pitched voice was so bad it would drive a coyote to suicide. Then I set out to find Ida Mae and try to apologize to her for what I'd said.

And to tell you the truth, I was so busy thinking about what I was going to say to her that I didn't even notice, until we were past, the dusty bay horse loping along about fifty yards east of the train.

Suddenly I saw him, shouted with joy, and began running through the train toward the front. That was Pa! We were going to make it! We had caught Pa!

Through the four cars I ran, doing my best to keep one eye on Pa while I watched where I was going with the other. I missed once, though, but I want you to know that I really didn't mean to knock the conductor down. Why, I even apologized as I jumped over his entangled body! In the front car I passed Ida Mae, but I had to get up to the tender and let Mr. Steiner know that I had to get off.

"Hyrum—" she said as I ran past. But I didn't have time to stop, not then.

"Later!" I shouted, and then I was out the door and scrambling up the tender. Only at that moment we entered the cut through the ridge south of Santaquin, and suddenly I could no longer see Pa.

Oh, no! I thought. How am I ever going to get his attention? How am I going to . . .?

Still scrambling, I made my way across the coal-filled tender and down into the engine, where I stood gaping. There was surely no comparison between this giant machine and the old Sanpete Crawler.

"Mr. Steiner, that was Pa back there, and—"

"Yes, son. I saw him. Looks to me like he is doing all right, too. He's near two miles ahead of those two galoots on the white mares. Now you just relax and keep out of the way. We'll be at the depot in no time."

"But, sir, that's just it. I've got to warn him *before* we get to the depot, not after. Ida Mae said her father wanted that woman to be waiting just over this ridge here, not down at the depot. She'll be laying in the trail, and Pa won't have a chance—"

"Well, why didn't you say so? I reckon I misunderstood when you and old Yergeson were jawing at me back in Nephi. Okay, boy, you're in charge. You say the word, and I'll hit the brakes."

"Uh . . . how long is this cut?"

"It ends just beyond this curve. Another fifty, sixty yards, I'd say."

"All right, stop it just the other side of the cut. That way I can run up the trail and maybe get there before Pa does."

"Sounds good. You need any help? I mean, can you run all right with that foot?"

Well, this time I really grinned, thinking instantly of Ida Mae. Bless her heart, she surely did have a way of making a feller take a good look at himself.

"No, sir. This old foot slows me down a little, but when I have to, I can get along pretty well. Just ask the conductor back there. Thank you anyway, Mr. Steiner, but what has to be done I want to do myself."

He grinned then and shook my hand.

"You'll do, boy," was all he said. "You'll do."

And then he pulled on the brakes. In another moment we'd be through the cut and I'd know if we were on time.

14

Enduring on the End

Pain Mumford leaned against the door-frame of the Aspen Wells Co-op, his body racked with a new spasm of coughing. He had been amazed at how his little fire had spread, and there had been a time when he wondered if he would get it out at all. But he had, and now he suffered from smoke inhalation, fatigue, and an overwhelming sense of guilt.

"Mungus," he gasped, tugging once again at his oft-used neckerchief. "I may not know much, but today I received a whole year's schooling in about five minutes."

"What you talking about, Pain?"

"The bishop, Mungus. I'm talking about our bishop. As far as I'm concerned, we had him all wrong. He'll do to ride the river with."

"Oh, no, don't tell me you didn't get the fire built! What'd you do, sleep in?"

"Hang it, Mungus! Stop yelling at me! I've enjoyed all the yelling from you I'm going to. I built your fires, and I was just getting them spread when here comes the bishop, pretty as you please on that big stallion. Right off he guessed what I was doing.''

"How do you know?''

"I know he knew! I've seen that twinkle in his eye before. He measures the doings of a man better than any bishop I ever had. And do you know what? Even when he knew what I was doing, he thanked me. Can you beat that? He thanked me for being up there on the job saving the town from fire. Funny thing is, he was right. As soon as he rode off the wind changed, and if I hadn't been there to put out that fire, if I'd run like a rabbit when I first saw him, why, Aspen Wells would have gone up in flames. And Mungus, that hay you cut last week—your whole crop—would have been the first thing to burn.''

"But the race? You didn't slow him down, Pain? Not at all? What about our money?''

"What's a hundred dollars, Mungus? Let me tell you something. It was worth a hundred dollars to me to learn what I did about the bishop today. To tell you the truth, I hope he wins.''

"Yeah, yeah, yeah. You sound like goody-goody Mumford all right. Today you really are a pain. Soderberg sure sucked you in. I can see that.''

"Maybe so, Mungus. Maybe so. And maybe he didn't, either. Maybe I'm just starting to see how bright the light is when you look out instead of in. You know what I think? I think you've spent too much time looking through the dusty fly-specked windows of the Co-op. Step outside, Mungus. Step outside and see how bright life can be when your conscience is clear and your mind is at peace.''

"You bet I'll step outside, you spineless traitor! I'll step outside with my boot planted on your backside. I'll mop up the street with you. I'll—''

"Mungus, why do you always think violence will solve your problems? That can only lead to trouble. One of these days someone will clean your meathouse, and I'll be there to hold his hat when he does it. Who knows? Maybe it will be me. Anyway, you make me tired. I'm going home.''

"Why, you—''

"Hold it, Mungus. Here comes more good news, I'll bet."

Sorenson brushed past Pain Mumford and into the street, concern clearly visible on his face. What had happened now? Why had his men returned so quickly? What was going on?

In a cloud of dust Anson Holman, Ollie Johnson, and Jesse Christensen plunged their horses to a stop, and Jesse leaped off and ran onto the boardwalk.

"Mungus," he coughed, clearing the dust from his throat. "Something went wrong. Something—"

"Oh, no!" Mungus groaned. "Not you, too? Why in heaven's name did I ever trust you numbskulls? Lay it out, Jesse. What happened?"

"I don't know, Mungus. Things were going just like you said they would. He passed us and we lit in after him firing and scaring him good, just like we were real outlaws. And the bishop was about ready to stop, too. We could tell. But then from out of nowhere came those two white mares you lost, crashing down on us so fast there was nothing we could do. We—"

"White mares? What are you talking about? I thought it was Soderberg who stole those mares."

"Yeah, so did we. But if he did, the men he gave them to turned against him real quick. Mungus, those two hombres were hard men, as cold-blooded as froze-solid rattlers. And they were shooting to kill, too."

"I'll say!" Anson groaned. "Look at this here hole in my arm, if you want proof. Mungus, those were real owl-hoots, men from up the river and over the pass. Those were Robbers' Roost boys if I ever saw any."

"Add it all up," Ollie joined, "and you'd have three dead partners right now, Mungus. We'd all be flybait except for one thing. They weren't really after us."

"Oh, yeah," Mungus growled. "And what makes you so sure of that? It sounds to me like you boys were taken out by Soderberg's own men."

"You're wrong, Mungus. Dead wrong. When we scattered, those fellows hardly even broke stride. We weren't there at all as far as they were concerned. They were after the bishop, and when we last saw them they were whooping and hollering and throwing lead at him like they were born to it."

"Yes, sir, Mungus. Unless Soderberg's stallion is a lot better critter than we think, your worries are over. Fact is, that's why we lit out of there. We didn't want our names linked in any way, any way at all, with the death of our bishop."

"Death!" Pain shouted. "Don't you boys believe it! It'll take more than you or anyone else has to kill that man!"

"Be quiet, Mumford! And get out of here! All the rest of you clear out, too. Some thinking's got to be done, and it seems to me I'm the only one with enough sense to do it."

Earlier, back in the canyon, the two outlaws had experienced similar frustrations.

"Whooaahh! Settle down now, you old mare! Confounded train! What in thunder is that engineer blowing his whistle at here? Crazy nag, ain't you ever heard a train whistle before?

"Blue John, you all right? I don't like saying this, but your face looks like the north end of a south-bound mule!"

Blue John staggered slowly to his feet, his head spinning as he reached up to adjust his hat. "Silvertip," he groaned, "what happened?"

"Your horse spooked, Blue John, and dumped you. That's what comes of never learning to fork a bronc. You and your wagons."

"So where's the horse?"

"Look quick, pardner, and you'll see it hightailing it over the ridge yonder."

"Oh, no! Where am I going to get another nag?"

"Beats the tar out of me," Silvertip replied caustically. "Fresh mounts in this canyon are scarcer than bird feathers in a cuckoo clock."

"Come on, pardner. Give me a hand up behind you. I'm so weak I'd have to lean against a fence post just to spit."

"Yeah, you look like it, too. But sorry, I ain't givin' you no ride, Blue John. I'll chase down your mare for you, but until I get it, you're afoot. You hoof it along after that Mormon bishop feller as best you're able, and I'll be back directly.''

"Say, Silvertip. You'd better be quick, and you'd better come back. We're both in this deeper than either of us wants to admit, and we've got to get that there stallion.''

"Why, Blue John, you surprise me. All this verbal lather you're working up makes me feel like you don't trust me. You get walking, and I'll be back with your mare before you top the next ridge.''

Nearly three hours later, and much further up the trail, a weary and saddle-sore Jons Soderberg forced his mount through a clump of willows and headed it up the gradual slope that led eventually over the ridge and into Santaquin Valley, a part of the larger Utah Valley. For the thousandth time he shifted his position in the saddle, trying to ease his aching muscles.

Forty miles, he thought, and still another seventy to go. How will I ever last?

"Heavenly Father,'' he sighed, "a couple of hours ago I was asking your help to win. Now I'm thinking that just getting there would do fine, no matter when it is. Lord, the scripture says we must endure to the end. But as for your old bishop here, he'd be satisfied if he could just endure *on* his end.

"Come on, Ingersol, you're doing fine. Once we get over this ridge it'll be downhill for you all the way to the Jordan Narrows. Here comes the Utah Central, big fella. Too bad we can't catch a ride. But that's fine, for in the morning we'll be riding it on our way home.''

A few minutes after the train had passed, the man and the horse topped out on the ridge. Pulling his mount to a halt to catch his breath, the bishop leaned back, lifted his canteen, and took a long pull at the warm water. Dismounting then, he took more water and splashed out the stallion's nostrils. Pouring more into his hat, he let Ingersol moisten his mouth.

"That's enough, old boy,'' he murmured softly. "Too much water and a run in this heat would kill you. We'll get you all the water you want in the stables in Salt Lake City. Until then, old horse, just trust me.''

Climbing back into the saddle, Soderberg glanced out over the valley. Suddenly he sat up in amazement. The train had stopped below him in the cut, and a few people were milling around outside. But what really surprised him was that not more than seventy yards away a fellow was kneeling in the trail, and that fellow looked an awful lot like his son Hyrum. In fact, that girl beside him certainly resembled Ida Mae Sorenson. There were three other men, too, but those he didn't know.

"What in thunder?" he growled as he slapped his spurs to his horse. "What are Hyrum and that Sorenson girl doing here? I left them back in Aspen Wells!"

15

The Dress or the Stain?

Leaping out the door and through the cloud of hissing steam, I raced up the hill toward where I knew that woman must be waiting for Pa to arrive. A pretty Appaloosa with its reins dragging was feeding on the grass above the trail, and I guessed that would be her horse. Knowing I must be close, I ran as fast as my leg would allow, and in no time I came huffing and puffing through the brush to almost stumble over the prone form of the woman. She was in the trail all right, just like Mungus had planned, and as I looked at her my heart went out to my Pa. How could one man survive so much opposition?

The woman's appearance startled me. She was small, smaller even than Ma, and besides that, she was probably the most beautiful woman I had ever seen—Ida Mae excepted, of course.

In the second I stood looking at her, I saw one eye blink open and glance at me, and then quickly close. And if I hadn't seen it I might have doubted that she was conscious at all. She surely looked to be hurting.

Kneeling down, I smoothed back her hair, and as I did so I heard Pa's horse come over the ridge above us and stop, blowing to catch its breath.

"Take it easy, Ma'am," I said softly, doing my best not to grin. "You're hurt real bad, but don't worry about a thing. I'll get you to the train."

"Hyrum," Ida Mae whispered, peering over my shoulder, "what are you doing?"

"This lady's hurt bad, Ida Mae. Her horse must have thrown her, and she looks to be busted up something awful."

"But Hyrum, she—"

"Now hush up, Ida Mae. She's hurt, and I'll take care of her. You gather up her things, and I'll carry the poor lady to the train."

At that moment three men rose up from the brush and started toward us, but knowing why they were there, I paid them no mind. I just reached down, gathered that woman up in my arms, and was turning toward the train when up galloped Pa on old Ingersol.

Instantly the woman opened her eyes. "Put me down, you young fool!" she hissed.

"Just relax, Ma'am," I said softly, making my voice as innocent as possible. "Don't worry about a thing. I'll carry you to safety."

"But you don't understand! I—"

"Hi there, Pa!" I shouted, drowning out the woman's frantic whisper.

"Hyrum, what in heaven's name are you doing *here?*"

"Got no time to explain, Pa. This woman's hurt bad, but, well . . . Ida Mae and I are taking care of her just fine."

"But—but—" Pa stammered.

"Pa, button your lip and trust your son. Those two hombres on Mungus's mares are already past Mona, and coming fast. These gents here don't appear any too friendly, either. Was I you, I'd slap spurs and light a shuck out of here. It's still a long way to Salt Lake City."

Well, right then Pa was without doubt the most muzzled and puzzled man in the Territory of Utah. But after about ten seconds of staring hard at me, he caught my drift, winked, slapped spurs, and was gone before those three men could say "Aye" or "Nay" or anything else, for that matter.

Quickly I turned and was starting through the brush toward the train when one of the men reached out as if to stop me. I sidestepped and twisted past him, but with an oath the others started for me. Well, talk about being in a pickle! I knew I couldn't outrun them, and with the woman in my arms there was no way that I could outfight them, either. Oh, what I would have given for a few of my brothers right then! It's times like that when a fellow realizes just how much of a blessing a family can be.

"Ida Mae," I said suddenly, "if these hombres take another step, you give a shout for Marshal Clawson. He told me to holler if I had any problems, and these fellers are shaping up to be a problem."

Well, my mentioning the marshal's name surely stopped them, and I reckon that was the first time that marshal ever helped us. It's too bad he wasn't there to see how well he did. It was easy to see that those three didn't want to believe me, but then they didn't dare not believe me, either. It was what I guess you'd call a Mexican stand-off. The big one, though—the man who'd first grabbed for me—was licking his lips, and I could tell by his eyes that he was getting ready. Marshal Clawson or not, he wanted another try at me. And if he got one I knew I was a goner. That gent looked mean enough to have a reserved seat in—well, in a very warm location.

Cautiously I backed up a step, then another, signaling with my eyes for Ida Mae to get over behind me. The woman in my arms was quiet, but I felt her body tense, and I knew she was going to move the same moment those other hombres did. But what could I do about it? I couldn't run fast enough to get away from them, and if I wanted to fight I'd have to put the woman down, which I didn't want to do, either. So I stepped back another step, got Ida Mae a little closer to me, and prayed a little harder. I could see no way out of this mess, no way at all.

The big man suddenly grinned and spoke, his voice so cold his jowls were dripping ice-water. "Boys," he said, "this young whippersnapper's bluffing us. Ain't no marshal on that train, is there, boy?

You and the little gal pull a good bluff, but not good enough! Drop that there woman now, 'cause we're about to tear you apart, and you'll need all the hands you got to defend yourself with."

Nervously I took another step back, looking for some way out. My hands were sweaty, and my mouth felt like cotton. I rolled my tongue around a bit, licked my lips, and wished I had enough moisture there to spit, to show them that I wasn't scared. Only I didn't, and I was. And there wasn't a thing I could do about it, either.

"Come on, boys," the big man said. "Let's get him!"

He took a step toward me, and out of the corner of my eye I saw the other two start forward at the same time. I was about to drop the woman and do my best to defend myself and Ida Mae when from behind me I heard a loud metallic click, the sound of a carbine lever action working a shell into a chamber.

Those old boys heard it, too, and they came to a mighty sudden halt. The big man was staring nervously over my shoulder, and I slowly turned to see the engineer, Cale Steiner, standing in the brush with his Model 1873 Winchester carbine .44-40 aimed right at the belly of one of the men to my side. Quickly I stepped back, and then Brother Steiner swung that rifle to bear on the big man who was obviously the leader.

"Was I you," Cale Steiner said casually, "I'd hoist my hands as high as they'll go. Quick, before I cut loose my dogs and make you as dingy as three head of sheep!"

Those six hands shot upright, and then Ida Mae lifted their hardware from them."

"Fine, Miss," Brother Steiner said. "Now, Hyrum, you take that woman down to the train where she can get proper aid. Miss, you take their weapons with you.

"Now you good ol' boys listen, because I'm only going to say this once. Keep your hands in the air, turn around easy-like, and mosey on back into that brush. I'm figuring to turn you loose, but one wrong move and you won't get loose for a long, long time. Savvy?"

They did, for they turned and marched off right regular-like, and Ida Mae and I made our way down to the train. Suddenly the woman spoke.

"Who are you?" she snapped. "And what are you doing this for? Put me down this instant!"

"Oh, no, Ma'am, I couldn't do that. You've been hurt far too badly to walk. Just you relax now. Your horse threw you back there on the trail, and you must have hit your head real hard. Otherwise you would remember what happened. My name is Hyrum, and this here is Ida Mae. Together we'll get you to some medical help as quickly as possible.

"Conductor!" I yelled, drowning out the woman's fumings and rantings. "I've got a woman here who's been hurt real bad. Would you get a place ready for her?"

Without waiting for a reply, I lifted her onto the coach, and did she ever put up a struggle! She was madder than a fumigated skunk. Right off, though, the train started, and by the time I got her fixed out all comfortable on the bench we were going so fast that she had no choice but to remain with us. I mean, only a dummy would ever think of jumping. Right?

"Take it easy," I said, making my voice as sympathetic as I could. "Lie still, and we'll get you to some help in no time. Ida Mae, come sit beside her while I go ask the conductor where the closest doctor is located."

Quickly I stepped back, and with a wink Ida Mae slipped onto the bench beside the woman, taking over swabbing her face with the damp rag someone had offered. In a moment three or four other people had gathered around, expressing sympathy, and then I knew we need worry no longer about what the woman might do. That little lady was trapped but good, and she knew it. Why, after all that sympathy had been shown, who would ever dare stand up and declare themselves a fraud? Nobody, that's who. At least not anybody I knew.

In the caboose I got a cup of water and took it forward to the woman, who seemed grateful for it. As she drank, her eyes bored into mine, but I just smiled back. And my smile was real, too, for I was about as happy as could be. After all, Pa was safe; and, by jimminy, I'd even helped him. Add that to the fact that I was spending the whole day with Ida Mae, we were no longer at odds with each other, and who could have been happier?

Gradually the people went back to their own seats, and after a few moments Ida Mae and I were alone with her once more. As I took the cup from her she asked once again who I was. I wasn't going to tell her, but Ida Mae took matters into her own hands, and before I could stop her, the truth was out.

"Don't you know?" she asked simply. "Why, Ma'am, this is Hyrum Soderberg, son of Bishop Jons Soderberg of Aspen Wells."

Well, you'd have thought someone had pole-axed the woman, the way she looked at me. First she turned white, and then she turned red, and for a moment there she was so perplexed I thought she was going to turn inside-out.

"Soderberg!" she gasped. "Then you knew? You knew all along that I wasn't—that I was in that trail to— Say, how much *did* you know?"

"About everything, I reckon. Ma'am, I knew you weren't hurt, and I knew that you were set out there to stop my Pa, too."

"Is that all?"

"Well, shucks. I—"

"If you know more, young man, tell me!"

"All right, Ma'am. Other than that all I know is what I've heard. And that is that those men who asked you to do what you were doing said some bad things about your . . . well, reputation, Ma'am. They said you would tear your blouse and try to destroy Pa, too, and that would end his career as bishop."

For a long time she was silent, and I was feeling pretty uncomfortable. I didn't want to hurt her, but she'd wanted me to be honest, and I had been.

"What you've said is true," she said finally. "But I don't understand how you could have known."

"I told him," Ida Mae said.

"You? And who are you?"

"This is Ida Mae Sorenson," I replied quietly. "She is Mungus Sorenson's daughter."

"Oh . . . merciful heavens, no!" she groaned.

"Ma'am," Ida Mae said. "My father is normally a good man. And I love him with all my heart. But right now he is trying, because he is jealous, to destroy our bishop, and that is not good. I love him too much to let him do that. If Mother was alive she'd have stopped him, but since she isn't, I'm the only one left. That's why I told Hyrum, so we could save his father, and hopefully mine, too. The bishop we had to save from you. Father we have to save from himself, and I'm sure that will be the hardest job of all."

"Well, I'll be switched," the woman said thoughtfully. "You two are really something. Do you know that? Do your fathers know what you are doing?"

"Pa does," I said. "At least he must be guessing right now, for he surely saw me back there in the trail. He's quick, and it won't take him long to put two and two together."

"Miss Sorenson?"

"No, my father and my brother don't even know where I am. There just wasn't time to tell them. Right now I'm probably in real big trouble."

"Yes, you might be, at that. But don't worry, you've done right, and right always works out for the best. Say, did you believe what you heard about my . . . er . . . reputation?"

Well, what could either of us say to that? Of course we believed it. We had nothing to tell us otherwise. So both of us dropped our heads and neither of us answered, and I reckon that was all the answer she needed.

"I see," she said, almost whispering. "But what could I expect? Neither of you know me. And besides, there I was, right in that trail, right where they said I'd be, doing just like they'd asked me to do. Oh, isn't life miserable when you set out to deceive people?"

And then she started to cry, not loudly, but just silently sobbing as if her heart were broken. Ida Mae slipped over and put her arm around the woman's shoulders, and that lady looked more like a little girl right then than anything else. Ida Mae was crying, too, and to tell you the truth I was fighting back a couple of tears myself. I mean, that little lady was really hurting.

Later, when she'd dried up a little and we were talking, she said something that I've never forgotten.

"You kids listen to me," she said, "and pay attention. Have you ever seen someone in a beautiful white dress who had a little spot of food or something spilled on it?"

We both nodded, and she continued.

"When you see someone who has something spilled on their white dress, what is it that you see, the dress or the stain?"

"Why, the stain."

"Right. You see the stain every time. And it doesn't matter how small the stain is, either. In fact, it's hard to keep your eyes off the stain. Now, remember, the same thing is true with a reputation. One spot on it, one blemish, and that's all folks will see. No matter how many good things there are about a person, all people can see is the one spot of dirt in their character. And, saddest of all, that's sometimes all that a person can see about herself, too. In fact, mostly we judge ourselves more harshly than others do. We take what they say about us, magnify it, and then judge ourselves accordingly. I'd been told I was bad so many times that I came to believe it. And since I have believed it, I have acted the part, and so it has become true. Thank you. Thank you so much for helping me to see through your eyes what I was. Run along now, both of you. I'll be fine. And I promise you that I will be no further trouble to either of you. Go on, go be together. Right now I'd say you deserve that."

Neither of us protested that idea, and without a word we stood, Ida Mae took my arm, and we walked away. And funny thing was, I never for one moment doubted that the woman had meant what she said. She had given her word, we believed her, and as it turned out we were right in doing so. But that is another story entirely.

As we walked toward the caboose I thought again of the fight we'd had earlier, and I knew that I needed to apologize to Ida Mae. After all, it was my pride that had caused it, and nothing else. On the platform back of the caboose we stood for a time in silence, staring out at the barren and steep slopes of Mt. Nebo rising to the east of us.

"Funny," I said, finally, "how pretty that old mountain can be when there's so little on it to actually make it pretty."

"Yes," she replied quietly. "It's a lot like some people I know. Their beauty runs much deeper than what can be seen on the surface."

"Ida Mae, I'm sorry. I—"

"I know, Hyrum. So am I."

And so we talked it out, and as we talked we were both grinning and we were holding hands and it was great, standing on that platform while the Utah Central rattled along toward Salt Lake City.

16

What, Him Again?

Hour after never-ending hour Jons Soderberg pushed his mount northward, skirting Spring Lake and Payson, and then riding through Benjamin and into Spanish Fork. As he passed the intersection of First East and Fourth South in Spanish Fork he couldn't help but re-experience the pain of that winter thirty years before when he had stood beside his elder brother, Peter, as they had buried Peter's first-born son. The baby had been born beneath the cottonwood that still stood on the southeast corner of the intersection. Their only shelter during that frigid month had been a draughty wagon box, for they were among the thirty thousand Saints forced to flee their homes when Johnston's Army—in what many were now calling Buchanan's Blunder—had marched against the Mormons back in 1857. Brother Brigham had assigned the members of the South Cottonwood Ward to relocate in Spanish Fork, a community established under his direction only eight years prior to the Utah War. The Soderbergs were among those so assigned. Jons himself, eleven years old at the time, had aided in the birth of his nephew that bitter freezing night in the wagon box beneath the skeletal branches of the cottonwood. Baby Peter contracted pneumonia almost immediately; within a few short days he was dead, and young Jons was experiencing for the first time the bitterness brought on by legal persecution.

How rapidly thirty years had passed, Jons thought, and how little had actually changed! Instead of being eleven, he was now forty-one. Besides burying a nephew he had now buried a daughter, and he was still being hounded by representatives of the federal government—and that in a country where the Constitution guaranteed it's citizens freedom of religion.

Pausing at Hobble Creek just south of Springville, Jons allowed the stallion a few moments' rest as he washed his face and refilled his canteen.

"Just halfway," he groaned aloud. "Ingersol, old boy, you might make it, but I'm not certain that I will."

As he rode down Center Street in Provo he wished there was time to pause for a quick lunch at the Dewdrop Restaurant, and thus give both him and his horse a much-needed rest. But there wasn't, so he nibbled his sandwich and pressed on, saddlesore and more weary than he had ever been in his life.

He crossed the Provo River and rode along the public works road his father and Peter had helped build during their first year in the Territory. Month after month they had traveled from Cottonwood to Provo to build that road, which was eventually pushed all the way into Heber Valley. The job had not paid money, but the men were given tithing scrip which they redeemed at the bishop's storehouse for the food they lived on that first season in the valley.

Both the bishop and his horse, though very tired, seemed to flow effortlessly as they passed through the high grasses on the bench and climbed the hill below Battle Creek. Lehi seemed to loom forever in the distance, but Soderberg knew that it was getting closer. He alternated his horse's pace, using all the skill he possessed, limited though that was, to spare his stallion. He thought about the men on the white mares, wondering where they were. He was certain they must have gained ground while he paused at Hobble Creek yet that rest had been beneficial for both himself and the horse. He could tell the difference in the way the animal moved, so for that stop he was glad. Yet he worried about the two men, and found himself hoping that they had passed him and would beat him into the city.

Once past Lehi the bishop could see in the distance the Jordan Narrows, and his mind drifted back to the summer of '58, the year Johnston's Army had established themselves at Camp Floyd. That summer Dan Bell, his deacon's quorum president, Terry Baker, the first counselor, and he had organized their first overnight, alone-without-adults excursion. It was a fishing trip to the Jordan Narrows where the large trout from Utah Lake could be caught. He recalled how his father had reluctantly consented to his taking the mare, giving in only when Baker, a head taller than himself, had accepted full responsibility for their safety. He recalled the fun they'd had, and wondered that fun should so often be reserved only for the youth. Why, in all the years since, he had never met anyone with the humor of Baker and Bell! "I wonder how Dan's doing," he thought, "homesteading over in Colorado." And Baker, too, in Los Angeles preaching the gospel at street meetings near an institution of higher learning which had been established there.

In his pocket Soderberg still carried the I*XL (I excel) Barlow-type pocket knife he had found that day in the Narrows. It had been brand new, and he remembered how proud he was when his father told him he would likely never own a better knife. That one, he said, was made in Sheffield, England, by a Mr. George Wostenholm. There was also a double-bladed knife, but the one he found was single-bladed, a perfect knife for the games of mumblety-peg he and the other boys were fond of playing. Again he wondered, as he had so often before, how his father had known the history of that knife, or, for that matter, how he had known any of the countless other things he always seemed to come up with. One of his neighbors, Dale Fielding, used to say that the bishop's father was as full of information as a mail-order catalog, and that was certainly true.

With a start the bishop realized that he had just passed the saloon that had once belonged to Porter Rockwell, and as he glanced back at it he was startled to see a cloud of dust not more than a half mile to his rear. Worse yet, within that dust he could see two white horses! Urging his horse to greater speed, the bishop lunged it across the ridge and into the Narrows, and there he was suddenly confronted with the sight of Marshal Clawson on his piebald gelding.

The marshal was still several hundred yards away, so hastily the bishop reined around and pulled back across the ridge, to be confronted again by the rapidly approaching horsemen. Which way now? Should he try to go up the ridge, which was terribly steep, or should he . . .?

"Hold up there, bishop!"

Taken back, Soderberg pulled rein, and there sitting on a rock just like before was the same old man he had spoken with in Salt Creek Canyon early that morning.

"Well, bishop, you are doing well, right well—considering. Another twenty-five miles, and you will have won!"

"Wha—why—how . . .?"

"Bishop, you're stuttering again. Had I known you stuttered, I might have taken care of that, too."

With that, the old man leaped sprightly to his feet, "Bishop, give me a hand. I need a ride."

"Wait a minute, old man. How in thunder did you get here?"

"Why, bishop, same as you. I traveled . . . quick! Now give me a hand up on that stallion of yours. We've got to hurry before those two highwaymen catch up with you."

"Highwaymen? What in . . .?"

"Ooops!" the old man grumbled. "Slip of the tongue. You call them outlaws now, I believe. Of course, it really shouldn't matter. They're the same breed now as they were back then. Still, if you don't give me a hand, those two whatever-you-want-to-call-thems back there will be on us for sure. Now, let's move!"

"I'm sorry, old-timer, but I've got to climb that ridge there, and I'm not about to carry double while I try to do it. I'm played out, my horse is played out, and I still have a good twenty miles to go before sunset. However you got here I don't know. I've seen so much today that I might believe anything. So, however you got here, you can get yourself away in the same manner. I'm leaving alone, so adios."

148

"Now, just a minute, youngster," the old man snorted. "Why aren't you going through the Narrows?"

"Because Clawson is in there, and I'm not about to let him get a hold of me."

"Do you want to get past him?"

"Certainly. But—"

"Listen up, bishop. You've been so deep in thought about the Utah War and that Barlow knife in your pocket that you haven't taken time to think about what's been going on around you. I'm not saying more, but if you don't lift me up on that horse you're never going to make it. You've got to hurry, man. You're being timed with a watch, not a calendar."

The bishop stared in amazement. How in blazes had this old man known all that, he wondered?

"Who are you, you old galoot?"

"Like I said before, young feller, names aren't important. I might be anybody. Now, how about that ride?"

Sensing the futility of further argument, and not a little concerned about who this old gentleman might really be, the bishop finally nodded. The old man seemed so doggone familiar. He looked a little like Jons's grandfather had looked, though there were differences, of course.

"All right," he said, holding out his hand. "Get on. But remember, it's mid-afternoon, and I'm setting no easy pace. I have no time to be troubled with an old man who is grumbling because of aches and pains."

"Don't you worry, bishop. I can't even remember the last ache or pain I had, unless maybe it's been since I began talking to you. But no matter—let's get through those Narrows."

"Old man, I've already told you that—"

"Bishop, get into those Narrows, and trust me, will you? I know that marshal considers you his number one wanted man, and I know he's sworn that he'll take you in. But do as I say, and you will have no trouble with him today. You won't even have trouble with the twenty men he has hidden on the hill behind him. Now ride!"

"Are you crazy?"

"Bishop!"

With that the old man slapped the stallion's rump, and they crossed the ridge again to ride directly toward Marshal Clawson and his hidden men.

"All right, friend," the bishop whispered as they drew nearer. "What am I supposed to do now? Doff my hat and ask Clawson if he wants to ride along with us?"

"Be quiet, you young upstart. You descendants are all alike . . . have to be shown everything. You have no faith, no faith at all. Be silent, now, and just keep riding. You keep your thoughts to yourself and they won't even know we're here."

"Oh, for Pete's sake," the bishop grumbled, not daring to argue further. Instead, he lowered his head, leaned forward in his saddle, and rode cautiously toward Marshal Clawson, expecting at any minute to be fired upon or arrested on the spot. But no, the closer he rode, the less attention Marshal Clawson seemed to be paying to him. When he was no more than fifteen feet away, he half-turned and whispered to the old man.

"What is it? Why can't he see us?"

"Sshhh," the old man whispered back. "Where did you learn to whisper? In a sawmill? He can't see us because he doesn't believe we're here. Don't you remember Paul in Second Corinthians saying if we don't have faith, we don't have sight?"

"No . . . but . . . say, that's not what he said!"

"Well, it's close enough! Now please be quiet!"

As they moved cautiously past Clawson and his deputies and up out of the Narrows, the only thing racing was the bishop's heart. Once on the rise above, however, he breathed a sigh of relief. And then with new-found courage he suddenly turned and shouted, "Say, Clodson, who're you looking for?"

"Oh, bishop!" the old man said reprovingly. "Must you always keep your mug filled with verbal lather? Aren't you ever going to learn that some feelings aren't meant to be spoken? Some thoughts ought best to be placed in a man's pocket and left there."

The bishop, not really listening to the old man, was grinning as he watched the marshal twisting this way and that, trying to determine which of his deputies had called him Clodson.

150

"Marshal Clodson," the bishop shouted, making his voice high and thin like an old man's, "do you still have mud in your mustaches, or did I clean it out that night at the dance in Aspen Wells? And how about that crooked pistol of yours? Did you clean the mud out of it yet?"

Several men stood up from the rocks to look around, and Marshal Clawson, his face livid with anger, turned his horse from side to side trying to see where the voice was coming from.

"Soderberg, blast your hide! Is that you? Where are you? Show yourself, you Mormonite coward! Show yourself, or I'll—"

"Relax, marshal. The reason you can't see me is—"

"Bishop," the old man interrupted, "say no more. The marshal will soon be busy, and I'm sure you'd rather be forgotten."

"Busy? But how . . . ?"

"Look back, bishop. Look back."

Suddenly there was a commotion of hoofbeats, and into the Narrows thundered Silvertip and Blue John astride the stolen white mares, now lathered and jaded, that were once the pride of Mungus Sorenson. Before they could stop, however, they were surrounded by a host of federal marshals.

"Well, well!" Marshal Clawson shouted heartily. "The telegram said two matching white mares, stolen from Aspen Wells and headed this way. Boys, have you got papers on those pretty broomtails?"

"Ah—well—ah—not with us, Mister," Blue John stuttered.

"Marshal to you, my friend. Your face looks familiar. Have you by chance been decorating the walls of any post offices lately?"

"Me? Why, Marshal, you must be joking. I'm as clean as the day I was born. Matter of fact, however, you have a right good eye. This gent sitting next to me is the notorious rustler and horse thief, Silvertip, straight from Robbers' Roost country. I captured him and these two fine fillies down by Nephi, and I was bringing them in."

"Why, Blue John, you dirty low-down no-account traitor! You'd sell your own mother and grin like a jackass eating cactus while you were doing it! I've a mind to—"

"Hold your tongues, you two," the marshal interrupted impatiently, "and right pronto you reach for some sky."

Just at that moment the Utah Central entered the cut and braked to a stop. Within minutes Ida Mae Sorenson and her unidentified escort had laid claim to her father's horses, and were carefully leading them up into the stock car, directly in front of the caboose.

"Well, bishop," the old man grinned, "what do you think of your son now? I hope you know that almost single-handedly he made possible your success in this race. That is quite the boy."

"Yes," the bishop admitted, "I'm beginning to realize that."

"Well, time surely does have a way of catching up with folks. doesn't it, bishop? It even does me from time to time. I think you'd best let me down now, as my errand is completed and it's time to get back."

With that the old man jumped lightly to the ground, where he stood, grinning still.

"Bishop," he beamed, "it's been a special pleasure making this trip with you. I can't remember when I've enjoyed an association so much. Now remember, keep working on your pride. Pay less attention to what folks say about you, and more to what you say about them. That will also solve your social pressure problems. And bishop, about those boys of yours—they need you, especially at this time in their lives. Most especially right now Hyrum needs you. You were pretty rough on him the other night after the dance. He was only saying what you've been saying to yourself all day long, and I expect a word of apology would go a long way with him. And, by the way, do you really think he should be restricted?

"Now, I'd best be going. We'll see you again, Bishop Soderberg."

"But wait! I still don't know—" the bishop called, and in that instant his mount shied to one side. For a second only his eyes were diverted, and when he looked back to finish his question, the hillside was empty. The old man was gone.

"Well, I'll be . . . !" exclaimed Jons Soderberg. "How'd that old galoot get down into that ravine so fast?" Then, without warning, something slapped his stallion on the rump, sending both horse and bewildered rider flying northward toward the valley of the Great Salt Lake.

17

Rubbing In and Reaching Out

Well, there isn't too much more to say about the race. Pa'd gone so long without eating that by the time he sat down to supper at the Beehive Restaurant in Salt Lake City, his stomach must have thought his throat had been cut. In the Temple-block stables, directly across the street north of the cemetery, stood Ingersol. Ida Mae and I were rubbing down and combing his giant frame, which was so ganted up that he looked like the running-gear of a grasshopper. Still, Ingersol had done his job, and now he was receiving his reward.

As we worked, the telegram, signed by fourteen brethren doing tithing work that day near the Temple block, was no doubt being circulated throughout Aspen Wells. It read simply:

> 7:15 PM ARRIVED SAFELY STOP SON HY AND IDA MAE SORENSON SAFE IN CITY STOP WILL LEAVE ON TRAIN TOMORROW AM FOR RETURN TO ASPEN WELLS STOP   SIG J SODERBERG BISHOP
>
> WITT J BRUCE PARKER   MERIDITH WILLIS

JD HAWKS   KENDALL JENSON
RUSS DAVEY   KARL QUILTER
DENNIS CARROL   DICK CHIDESTER
JERRY JEX   JIM OCKEY
MAX WALTERS   DAVE CONNALLY
R THOMAS BAILEY   DENNIS GIBBONS

That night Pa got hotel rooms for us, and after I said goodnight to Ida Mae I went to our room and found Pa reading the *Deseret Evening News*. I sat down and waited, wanting to talk and yet not wanting to because I was kind of afraid. I reckon Pa was scared, too, or else he had a busted talk-box, because that night he didn't talk about much of anything. I wanted so badly to tell him that I was sorry for being rude, but every time I tried the words just wouldn't come. I was surely feeling miserable. Then Pa asked me if I'd join him in prayer; I did, and when we finished he said goodnight and we went to bed. For a long time, though, I couldn't sleep. My mind kept going over the events of the previous few days, worrying them like a dog worrying a bone. Finally, when I was certain that sleep would never come, it did.

It was mid-afternoon the following day when the Sanpete Valley Crawler chugged into the depot at Aspen Wells. The trip home was largely uneventful, except for when Loose-lip climbed aboard in Nephi. When he saw us I thought he was going to have a consumptive fit, but he made it into another car and we never saw him again. For some reason Pa still didn't want to talk about the events of the preceding day, so instead he mostly sat while Ida Mae and I visited and got better acquainted. I'd never seen Pa so quiet, and to be right honest I didn't know what to think of him. It seemed a real switch that I would want to make medicine and he wouldn't. Normally Pa was a real speechifier.

As we stepped from the train in Aspen Wells we were surprised by the huge crowd gathering to meet us. It was Pain Mumford who first stepped forward to shake Pa's hand, but he had scarcely done so when Mungus pushed his way forward. Immediately Ida Mae ran to him, pleading, but he shoved her aside as though she were a stranger, reached up, and pulled Pa off the landing.

"Well, if it isn't our good bishop—good 'thieving' bishop, that is! Look hard, folks, for here before you stands the man who stole my white mares and then used them as he relayed himself toward Salt Lake City. Well, bishop, go ahead! Deny it!"

"Father!" Ida Mae screamed, climbing to her feet and running to her Pa once more.

"Father, that isn't so! I saw it! I—"

Mungus threw her aside again and turned back, snarling at Pa.

"Soderberg, you low-down—! Turned my own daughter against me, have you? I'll learn you to—"

And with a howl of rage he lashed out like a coiled rattler, his fist landing solidly on Pa's face.

Pa spun to the earth, and the crowd, suddenly silent, parted to give the two men room. Shaken, Pa rose slowly to his feet and held out his hand toward Mungus.

"Brother Sorenson," he coughed, wiping his blood from this cheek with the back of his hand, "as a bishop, I can't fight—"

With an oath Mungus swung again, and once more Pa was knocked to the ground.

Well, I felt sick, and I glanced over at Ma to see her face as white as a sheet. Why wasn't Pa fighting back? Was he a coward? Sure, he was bishop, but Mungus had taken it to him, had hit him first! And it shouldn't matter that Mungus was bigger, either. Pa could take him! Pa was strong enough, I knew that. I could see Jim and Lyman, and they were so anxious to get into it that they could hardly control themselves. Ma could, though, and she had. Those brothers of mine, badly as they wanted to participate, were going to be bystanders, and they knew it. And for that matter, so did I, for Ma had given me the eye, too. Still, I knew just how they felt.

"Pa!" I yelled. "Hit him back! Get up and . . . !"

Pa was starting to get to his feet again when Mungus stepped over and kicked him, a solid boot to the ribs that sent Pa rolling. For a moment he lay still, groaning, and the crowd, stunned, said nothing as Mungus moved forward to kick him again.

Suddenly the voice of Pain Mumford broke the silence.

"Hold it right there, Sorenson! That's it. Now back up a little, real easy. That's the way. Fair fights I don't mind, and mostly I leave a man alone to skin his own cats. But Mungus, that man is a bishop, and he's made him some promises that you and I don't even know about. So this forty-five says you'd best back off until he gets on his feet and decides what he's going to do."

Mungus didn't like it, but he looked hard at Pain and then took a step back, and then another. By that time Pa was on his knees right in front of me, staring off up the canyon. Then he said something so low that I could hardly hear him, and I doubt that many others heard anything.

"Old man," he said, gazing off up the canyon, "whoever and wherever you are, I'm thankful for your help. Yesterday morning you said to treat Mungus fair but firm. Until today I've been more than fair. Starting now I'm going to be more than firm. I hope you're watching!

"Pain, thanks for your help. I'm all right now."

Pa rose to his feet and beckoned for Mungus. "Sorenson," he said, "before I teach you some manners I want you to know that your mares were stolen by two outlaws from Robbers' Roost. They were captured by Marshal Hebron Clawson. Your daughter Ida Mae has them in the stock car with Ingersol, which horse I had the privilege of riding all the way."

With that, Pa hit him. It was so sudden that Mungus wasn't expecting it, and the blow knocked him flat. Rising quickly, however, he circled, feinted suddenly, and threw a hard right at Pa's head. Pa moved under it, though, and smashed a wicked left to the ribs that made the bigger man gasp.

Well, what followed, if it wasn't pretty, was at least quick. Pa wasted no time, and it was soon evident to all of us that he knew what he was doing. Somewhere, sometime, Pa had been up the river and over the pass, and I don't reckon any of us was more surprised to learn of that fact than Mungus, who found himself tied in a knot and hung out to dry on a bob-wire fence.

Mungus fought hard, I'll give him that. But it seemed like whatever he thought of doing, Pa was ahead of him. One time only Pa was hit, but he shook his head, mumbled something about firmness, and that was the last time Mungus touched him.

Two quick jabs to the face, a roundhouse to the midsection, and when Mungus's head jerked forward it met with Pa's knee, which was rising to the occasion.

Mungus went down with a long sigh, and Pa stood there for a moment, head bowed, and the absolute stillness of the crowd was profound. Suddenly, through cracked and bleeding lips, Pa spoke.

"I'm wondering, folks, if there are any others among you who need a dose of this medicine. If there are, step forward. Loose-lip, how about you?"

Loose-lip mumbled something, stepped back into the crowd, and then no one spoke, no one moved. Then Pa turned to me.

"Hyrum, come here. You too, Ida Mae."

Surprised, Ida Mae and I walked out to where Pa was standing. He was a mess of sweat and blood and dirt, and I noticed that he was rubbing his torn knuckles. The people were so silent that the sound of a horse snorting somewhere beyond the crowd startled me. As I drew near I could hear Mungus moaning softly, but Pa was ignoring him, and so did I.

As I got to Pa he put his hand on my shoulder and spun me around so that our backs were to the train and we were facing what was almost our whole ward. Ma, I saw, had moved over to stand by my brothers, and I could tell by their faces that they were as nervous as I was. What did Pa want, I wondered? Why would . . .?

"Brothers and sisters, for the past week or so I have been acting mighty strange for a man in my position, racing horses, betting, fighting, being prideful, and, worst of all, distrusting those who love me. In all that time only two people have had the courage to flat-out tell me that I was wrong—my wife Hattie and my son Hyrum. Because they had that courage I was rude to both of them, but especially did I mistreat Hyrum.

"During the race Hyrum continued to show courage, but it was then that he showed something even greater than that. He showed—

not just to me, but to all of us here—a sincere forgiving compassion for a father who had wronged him. And Ida Mae Sorenson did the same.

"You see, folks, he and Ida Mae accepted the responsibility of righting the wrongs each of their fathers had done, and of protecting them from themselves and from each other, forgiving them both beforehand.

"Brothers and sisters, it is this willingness to forgive and to accept responsibility, not only for one's own actions but for the actions of others as well, that is the measure of a man, and of a woman.

"Hyrum, you are a man I am honored to stand beside. And, Ida Mae, in every way you are a fine woman. Will you both forgive me?"

Well, I looked up at Pa then, he looked down at me, my eyes got all misty, and before I knew it Pa and I had our arms around each other for the first time in a lot of years. We were both crying and I don't remember when I felt so proud of being Pa's son. For a time neither of us could talk, and then Pa told me he loved me. I'd never heard him say it like that before, and suddenly I knew he did, and I knew I never need doubt it again. For a long time then nobody moved, and I just enjoyed being held by my Pa.

"Hyrum," he finally said, when we'd both dried up a little, "go fetch me some water, will you, please?"

I did so, and then with all those people watching, Pa knelt down, took out his neckerchief, and began cleaning Mungus's face. He was still fighting emotions, but as he cleaned he spoke again.

"Brothers and sisters, I won that race fair and square. That means thirty-five of you owe me one hundred dollars each, and Loose-lip, you owe me two hundred. The ward clerk will begin collecting that money tonight."

Pa paused, totally serious, and looked around the crowd. Most of them were shocked, and to tell the truth, so was I. Pa was not a betting man, and I had been fairly certain, after what he'd just said, that he would cancel the debts they owed him. But no, he hadn't, and when I looked at Ma she seemed about as sick as I suddenly felt.

"Add my hundred dollars to that," he continued, "and that will give us three thousand eight hundred dollars toward our new meetinghouse fund. With that much, I reckon we can break ground as soon as this problem between the Church and the government is taken care of.''

Suddenly, and without warning, Tucker Bill doffed his hat, waved it in the air, and called for three cheers for Pa.

The people roared, and while they did I just stood there wiping my eyes and grinning at Ida Mae.

Within minutes most of the folks had gone, and Pa and my brothers were helping a battered but clean Mungus Sorenson to his feet.

"Hyrum," Pa said, "come here, son, and help me support this man.

"Mungus, put your arms around our shoulders and we'll get you home in time for chores.''

"Say, bishop," Mungus groaned as we moved slowly down the street, "what'd you hit me with, anyway?''

"Righteous wrath, Mungus. Pure righteous wrath.''

"Was that true, what you said about my mares?''

"Father," Ida Mae interrupted, "the bishop wouldn't lie to you. You know that.''

"No," Mungus grimaced, "I suppose he wouldn't. But young lady, that brings me to you. Just whose side have you been on, anyway?''

"Your side, father. I've never been on any side but yours.''

Mungus was silent then, thinking about what his daughter had just told him, I reckon. Then, after a long minute, he spoke again.

"By golly, Ida Mae, you're right. I reckon it's about time I admitted that it was me who was on the wrong side.

"Bishop, how in tarnation did you get past all those traps I laid out for you? And why didn't you tell those folks back there what I'd done?''

"Mungus," Pa grinned, tightening his grip on the larger man's shoulder, "those are two good questions. Ida Mae and Hyrum helped me past one or two of the traps, and on the others I had help, too. I'm not saying who, and I'm not saying how, but I had some very special help. Now to answer your other question, I didn't tell them because I didn't think they needed to know. You're a good man, Brother Sorenson, and I feel strongly that the Lord would like to use your leadership abilities in his kingdom. Mungus, will you accept a call from your bishop?''

Mungus stuttered and stumbled and choked and coughed, and I was wondering what in the world Pa was trying to do. But then Mungus looked over at his daughter, she smiled and winked at him, he stood straight and tall (or at least he stood as straight and tall as he could, considering his recent shellacking by Pa), and turned to Pa.

"Bishop Soderberg, I'd consider that a real honor. I surely would."

They both grinned then, and resumed their slow walk down the street.

"Say," Mungus interjected, "that must have been a heck of a horse race, bishop. Some day I'd like you to tell me about it."

"Some day I will, Mungus. Some day I will."

The two men leaned on each other then, walking arm in arm, and I dropped back to walk with Ida Mae. Taking my arm, that young lady looked up, and, with tears in her eyes, she said simply, "Oh, Hyrum!" Then she leaned up and kissed me, and, by jimminy, this time it was special, this time it was right.

Funny thing, though. Right as it was, that kiss discombobulated me so badly that my tongue got hog-tied and I couldn't make chin music at all, so I just held on tight to Ida Mae and kept walking, doing my best to follow in the footsteps of my Pa.